D0891268

Sad Old
FAGGOT
SKY
GILBERT

a misFit book

Published by ECW Press
665 Gerrard Street East
Toronto, ON M4M 1Y2
416-694-3348 / info@ecwpress.com

This is a work of fiction. Names, characters,
places, and incidents either are the product
of the author's imagination or are used
fictitiously.

Purchase the print edition
and receive the eBook free!
For details, go to ecwpress.com/eBook.

LIBRARY AND ARCHIVES CANADA
CATALOGUING IN PUBLICATION

Gilbert, Sky, author
Sad old faggot : a novel / Sky Gilbert.

ISBN 978-1-77041-310-8
also issued as: 978-1-77090-927-4 (PDF)
978-1-77090-926-7 (ePUB)

1. Title.

PS8563.I4743S22 2016   C813'.54
C2016-902355-9   C2016-902356-7

Editor for the press:
Michael Holmes/a misFit book
Cover design: Rachel Ironstone
Cover image: © Liam Sharp

The publication of *Sad Old Faggot* has been generously supported by the Canada Council for
the Arts which last year invested $153 million to bring the arts to Canadians throughout the
country, and by the Government of Canada through the Canada Book Fund. *Nous remercions
le Conseil des arts du Canada de son soutien. L'an dernier, le Conseil a investi 153 millions de
dollars pour mettre de l'art dans la vie des Canadiennes et des Canadiens de tout le pays. Ce livre est
financé en partie par le gouvernement du Canada.* We also acknowledge the Ontario Arts Council
(OAC), an agency of the Government of Ontario, which last year funded 1,709 individual
artists and 1,078 organizations in 204 communities across Ontario, for a total of $52.1 million,
and the contribution of the Government of Ontario through the Ontario Book Publishing Tax
Credit and the Ontario Media Development Corporation.

PRINTED AND BOUND IN CANADA   PRINTING: WEBCOM   5   4   3   2   1

"Those who didn't understand will never understand: disco was much more, and much better, than all that. Disco was too great, and too much fun, to be gone forever! It's got to come back someday. I just hope it will be in our own lifetimes."

— *The Last Days of Disco*

for Ian

How Should a Faggot Be?

I found a worm in my bed.

I was checking because we got this notice about bedbugs in our building. Christ, I don't even like to think about them crawling all over me.

There's a painting at the MLT in downtown Toronto — you know the MLT, the Magic Lantern Cinemas? They sometimes show art there and they have a piano and it's really very, you know, friendly.

I'm sure it won't last long.

Anyway the painting — it's more of a drawing really — is of a woman with little bugs crawling all over her. The artist who made it is fucking lousy. I say that because I can tell it's meant to be artistic . . . pretty . . . whatever. I mean for anyone who has ever had bugs crawling all over them (and I have — there *were* bedbugs in our apartment once) it's hard to look on a painting like that as "artistic."

Anyway I was tearing the sheets off the bed and searching for bedbugs and at the end of the bed in one of the ridges in the corner of the mattress where you usually find bedbugs I found a little worm.

It was writhing in the sunlight.

It was probably dying.

Or who knows — it could have been wriggling around having a gay old time thinking about its happy worm future. Who knows?

Anyway, it freaked me out so much that I just flicked it off the bed and onto the floor. Which was a dumb thing to do because after that I never saw it again. I think it might have been not a worm, but the larvae for some creature. Some creature that could grow into something big and buggy and eat me.

Jesus.

~

So, I'm going to tell the truth about Sky Gilbert. The whole truth and nothing but the truth. I know you've heard that before, and you've also heard many a doofus question "What is truth?" But when they say shit like that you know you're getting the wool pulled over your eyes. Look in the toilet bowel. Look at your asshole in a mirror, that's truth. Everything else is salad dressing.

Sure you can challenge me — what do I mean when I say my truth? And I would say: what I know about myself for sure. I'm going to tell all here, though I'm not going to trash people. I mean there are obviously some people I can't talk about — mostly because I don't hate them. That's the trouble with a book like this. You end up sounding like a crank. (I am a crank, and that's the truth.) I can't write about the people I love except to say I love them. So when I get to someone I love I'll just say "I love them." Which means I'm not going to talk about them in any detail. Because, truth be told, there are of course things I don't like about them, even though I love them. But I love them too much to tell you those things.

You just have to accept that. Or at least accept the fact that I'm telling you the truth.

This book isn't going to be like the one I wrote 16 years ago called *Ejaculations from the Charm Factory*. That was a "memoir" about my life up to the age of 46. I'm not going to say that the book was a lie. But it was certainly very carefully calculated. My editor Michael Holmes came to me with the idea of a memoir and at first I didn't want to do it because I figured I'd have to tell the whole truth and alienate a lot of people whom I still loved. But Michael said, "Hey, you can be very strategic about what you write and what you don't."

So that's exactly what I did. That book is not the truth about me. In fact it is the furthest thing from the truth in some ways. I like to say that it's the facts about me but none of the inner truth. I only said nice things about my friends and I picked very specific people to trash. Only people I really hated at the time. For instance I really let Kyle Rae have it. And the Good Reverend Brent Hawkes. That was very calculated — in the sense that I thought not only that those two people deserved my hate but that it wouldn't hurt my career to trash them. I wasn't, for instance, going to trash Tim Jones — so I tried to minimize the conflict we had when he was my general manager at Buddies in Bad Times Theatre — because I knew he was becoming a powerful arts executive. And even though I knew really scandalous gossip about *Toronto Star* theatre critic Richard Ouzounian, I didn't want to put that into the book because he was, well, a big deal at that time.

Now I'm not saying that my memoir is a piece of shit. I still think it has some value as a document about growing up artistic in the crazy Queen Street of Toronto in the '80s. But as a fucking *memoir*, who cares? When it comes down to it, who gives a shit about me in the grand scheme of things?

So what the fuck am I doing here? If my story doesn't matter then what's the point of me writing *another* book about me? Well, the inspiration came from an article by Susan Swan I just read in the *Globe and Mail*. I'm ashamed to say I've never read a book by Susan Swan. I've read hardly any books by Canadian authors, period. Sorry about that. I mean I used to like Margaret Atwood and Robertson Davies when I was a teen. But basically, it's like this. I start in on a Canadian novel and it doesn't take long before I just get bored and disappointed. I recently really tried to read Lynn Coady. It started out great, then . . . I just lost interest. I don't mean to trash Lynn Coady especially. She seems a lot better than the rest. (I read nearly half the damn thing.) I mean it really was readable . . . whatever. I can't remember the title. It had a good title, and the book was funny but . . . I don't know. I apologize for not being more Canadian.

But I do know who Susan Swan is and she seems to me to be very smart and beautiful (even if she's old like me).

The article was a review of some Swedish writer whom I will probably never read so forget about him. But in the article, Susan Swan talks about the "new novel" and how the new novel is not fiction but biography. And she uses Sheila Heti's book *How Should a Person Be?* as an example. The gist of her argument is that the "new" novelists are better because they reveal so much about themselves, their real actual lives. They write fact, not fiction, or at least mix the two together in heavy doses. And you can't measure a novel by how "imaginative" it is, but by how much it actually reveals about the author's life.

Okay, so I read that. And I thought, hey, I can do that.

Probably better than fucking Sheila Heti.

Don't get me wrong, I've got nothing against Sheila Heti. I met her twice. I think she is fucking gorgeous, for sure. If I was straight I would totally be in love with her. Totally. She reminds me of a thin version of Lena Dunham — and honestly, isn't that what everybody wants to be? She's obviously very delicate and sensitive and smart as a whip. I met her at Hillar Liitoja's house — he's a director friend of mine and she was on the board of his theatre company. Sheila was very polite to me but we didn't bond until we ended up at a donor's dinner together for another little theatre company. Then we let loose and gossiped and had *so* much fun. I was *completely* charmed by her.

So I'm seriously jealous now because she is the greatest novelist since sliced bread and I'm not.

But really I have nothing against her. It's not about Sheila Heti being awful, it's about me being awful for being so small-minded as to be jealous of her.

And the only reason I think I could do this whole "reality novel" thing better than Sheila Heti is because of this: it's easy to be a reality novelist when you are young and beautiful and brilliant and have your life before you, and the biggest problem you have ever faced is breaking up with Carl Wilson.

Okay, this is the thing. I've never even met Carl Wilson, but he published an article of mine once and I've talked to him on the phone. And he strikes me as one of the most brilliant and sensitive males on the face of the fucking earth. *I* would like to marry him (and I don't want to marry anybody). And he was Sheila Heti's partner.

I'm sure most straight women would kill to have had Carl Wilson as a lover or husband or even just a one-night stand. I read Carl Wilson's book about Celine Dion called *Let's Talk About Love* and I just fucking adored it. (Okay, so I *did* like one recent Canadian book.) Now the truth about that book is — and I'm not telling tales out of school because Wilson admits as much — *Let's Talk About Love* is all about Sheila Heti. That's why I love the book so much, because it's a love letter in the form of an essay. Read between the lines — Wilson keeps digressing and talking about Heti — and the book is up there with Roland Barthes *A Lover's Discourse* as far as I'm concerned. It's a theoretical book that is actually driven by a real love affair.

Wow.

So what I'm saying is that Sheila is young and beautiful and brilliant with her whole life ahead of her and has only had the singular misfortune of being loved too much by a perfect, brilliant man.

So who wouldn't want to read a reality novel about her charmed fucking life?

And me, I'm an old, crippled faggot. I'll never run again. I'll never kneel again — not without help — very humiliating, let me tell you, for an old cocksucker like me. I'm 62 years old and I drink too much and I'll probably be dead soon. And I'm still a fucking hopeless (and I mean it is hopeless) slut.

The real truth about Sheila Heti is one thing.

But who wants to hear the real truth about me?

What It's Like
Being Sky Gilbert

~

I know it's really hard to get into anybody's brain and live there, but I'm going to try and give you some idea of what it's like being me.

I am one really sad, lonely, old faggot.

First of all, I've always just generally been sad. I cry a lot. Or at least a lot for a man. I even *like* crying, which suggests to me that I am essentially a sad person. My favourite thing to do is to put on an opera or a piece of romantic music and get all misty-eyed. It's irrelevant what kind of music it is — mostly stuff that other people reject as too pretty or light-weight (Donizetti, Bellini). Or music written by fascists like

Richard Strauss or by sad-eyed Russians like Rachmaninoff. Yes, I actually like his Piano Concerto no. 2, and it always cheers me up to have a good cry over it.

But I don't know if I'm convincing you, because even as I'm writing this I'm thinking, wow, it sounds like crying is a good time for me. So that makes me happy, not sad.

But I don't think that's true.

I think you can get a good insight into me if you think about a certain piece of music that someone once suggested reminded them of me. It was a '70s power ballad called "All by Myself," and it was all about some lonely guy who is saying he doesn't want to be all by himself anymore. I can't remember who sang it. But the song was actually set to the music of the second movement of Rachmaninoff's Piano Concerto no. 2. I can't remember who recommended that piece of music to me. But let's just say that after the person said, "This song reminds me of you," I cheerily went out and bought the damn thing and it was like getting hit with a ton of bricks. The song is probably the most depressing, lonely song ever written. In fact I couldn't listen to it anymore after the first time because it just reminded me too much of myself — if that makes any sense at all.

My loneliness seems to have originated with my homosexual desires. I spent years and years growing up being alienated and writing in little journals, trying not to be attracted to boys and just trying to be straight and fuck women (which I did until I was 30 years old, still nearly half my life). Of course I thought I was evil and I couldn't tell my parents, and I disapproved of my desires, and all around me kids were having fun and dating and falling in love and I was so busy feeling bad about myself for having gay feelings that I couldn't even get attracted to other guys or fall in love with them. I was just lonely and separate and unhappy. I used to read Ayn Rand and imagine I was Howard Roark. The whole bit.

And then when I got older and became more well known in my career, I got popular, in the sense that my name was in the papers, but it didn't matter to me deep down because even though I was deluding myself, somewhere inside me I still liked to believe that maybe I was being loved for "me" — whatever that is.

But you know what? If you want to know the truth, there's not much *me* to love.

I don't mean physically. I weigh over 200 pounds and I have a pretty flabby belly.

What I mean is that now I know that I'm not a very nice person. (It's a difficult thing to have to say about yourself, but there it is.)

Basically I realize my *modus operandi* is that I'm essentially a performer, an achiever, and I want to be loved for my performances and my achievements, but I really haven't the faintest clue how to act on a one-to-one basis with anyone. I mean I can do it, but it's really tough.

For years I tried to make friends and I ran around trying to be popular. I used to agonize because I didn't have enough friends, and I was always losing friends and having to find more, and feeling that my life wasn't filled up enough with people, and fearing being lonely and alone. And now I've kind of given up. I've finally realized that people don't like me because I'm selfish, uncaring, and I don't want to be friends with them in the sense of caring for them and listening to them. I just want them to clap for my entertaining stories.

And unfortunately, at 62, it's a bit too late to develop a caring personality.

So I'm lonely but I've created that loneliness. I've created it because truth be told, I don't really want to be around people or put up with the trouble of being their friend (I only want to listen to them if they are really smart and entertaining — which is what I perceive myself to be) so I get what I deserve, which is like no friends at all.

I mean I have one or two. But I know even they will dump me, eventually. I'm basically in the position that my fucked up parents taught me that I was special, brilliant, and talented, and that I should get lots of love for it. So I do everything I can to get that attention, including writing play after play and book after book, but I can't really get anything other than applause from people because I'm essentially a performer, not a real human being.

I know this sounds very Faye Dunaway of me, but it's all true.

That's sort of the story of my life. The curtain always falls on the play, the novel always gets written. Not many come to see the play, not many people read the novel, but I get the odd review that says I was brilliant or at least entertaining. So I cherish those words while at the same time I go to bed lonely and alone and wish that more people liked me, the real me, not the entertaining gibberish that sometimes comes out of my mouth and that I provide in a desperate effort to keep people around.

And it would be all fine and good for me to say that I want to change and be a better person, but (I hate repeating this) I'm 62 years old, and never mind *can I,* at this late stage do I actually *want* to change? Will I be able to? To quote Bette Midler in her fabulous song: "Why Bother?"

And if I'm quoting Bette Midler here, you get some idea of how sad and fucked up I really am.

My Dick

~

I want you to have a really good picture of me, the real me, so I'm going to tell you about my dick. You probably don't want to hear about it, and believe me there's not very much that's exciting about it, so I'm not bragging. But not enough men talk to you about their dicks. I mean, of course, in a way they do because everything is about their dicks — the whole world is — in the sense that men are always telling you how fabulous they are, and how powerful they are, and how sexy and potent they are and all that shit.

But when it really comes down to actually talking about their actual penises, most men don't.

Why?

Because we're all ashamed.

Most of us don't have thick 10-inchers, that's why.

But on the other hand, most of us men spend most of our lives chained to our fucking dicks in one way or another — in the sense that we're always jerking off outside or inside somebody (which is really all fucking is, sometimes), so you'd think we might actually talk about our actual dicks for a change.

My dick is not very big when it's not hard. It's like a little acorn. It sits on top of my plump ball sack — I have one of those ball sacks that kind of looks like one plump, big ball — all curled in on itself with a bit of floppy foreskin covering it.

It kind of looks like a fat man's little dick, which is kind of what it is.

I should explain the foreskin part.

It's a very long story but I am circumcised. The thing is that when I was about 10 years old a doctor had a look at my foreskin and went crazy and said that I had been badly circumcised and that I might need to be circumcised again. So the truth is that I have a little too much skin for a circumcised man, and when my dick is not in a state of "excitation" it basically curls up into a little, barely inch-long, blob of skin.

When I get an erection then I'm about six inches long, maybe six and a half — I'm frankly afraid to measure it. I think one day I did measure it and it was almost seven inches, but I was really pressing the ruler down to the very base of my cock — so could we just say I'm average?

Now the truth is, I've never had any complaints. Though I have a lot of men at the baths take one look at it, notice it's not a 10-incher, then leave.

But if they do decide to give me a blow job, they really love it. I can understand that. I think that dicks can be beautiful, and I think it's a beautiful dick.

It has some nice throbbing veins that seem to get more pronounced as I get older (one of the few advantages of getting older) and it has quite a pronounced head, meaning that the head of my penis is slightly bigger than the shaft and there's a nice pronounced ridge around the head that sticks out above and around the shaft. And it's a pretty thick shaft. Not very thick, but pretty thick. (I'm not going to give you a measurement.)

The main issue I have with my dick is that it's so small when it's not erect. So if I'm at the bathhouse trying to get laid I have to masturbate basically all the time in order to make it presentable. And then when guys do start giving me a blow job they soon figure out two important things which tend to discourage them. First, the semi-hard dick I'm displaying doesn't really get much bigger even if it gets fully hard (which is sometimes a disappointment for the guys who are size queens). And second, nowadays especially, I sometimes don't really *get* hard.

Now on the one hand, that's not as big a deal as it sounds.

First, I'm not really into getting blow jobs, and I don't really like my dick being paid much attention to. (That's getting into my sexual habits, which is another thing altogether.) So frankly, I could give a fuck if they want to blow it or not. I'd rather blow *them*. And — related to this — basically I'm not that much into doing things sexually that require a hard dick. So I don't really give a fuck if my dick doesn't get as hard as it used to. But a limp dick is bad sometimes because some really cute guys require a hard dick even if they are not into getting fucked, but then some really cute guys couldn't give a shit whether your dick is hard or not.

However, I still come a lot, and often.

I'm into coming.

My Ass

Since we've talked about my dick, we might as well talk about my ass. Flip me over, so to speak. What I really mean to talk about here is my asshole — but I figured if I called this chapter that, then no one would read it.

I have always had a pretty nice ass. That is, it's big and round and white and it has been — up until recently — firm. Now it's getting saggy and wrinkly a bit (especially at the top of my legs).

Then there's my asshole. What's interesting about my asshole is that it is a) so tight and b) buried very deep within my ass cheeks. What I mean by that is that there is quite the distance between the cheeks of my ass and my actual hole.

I also have a bit of a dirty asshole. This is a problem because if you want to get fucked (which I basically don't) you of course want to be clean. I must clean my asshole twice a day with warm water and soap, so I do everything I can to keep my asshole clean. In fact I'm obsessed with it. But, as they say in romance novels — to no avail.

And I could certainly do with a good bleaching. I've never been able to get away from having a little bit of a brown asshole, even though I do everything I can to clean it. And it's somewhat hairy around the hole, even though I am not basically very hairy at all.

And then there's the tightness of it. My wrinkly little sphincter is extremely tight, so much that I recently got the "You're so tight" from some guy. I'm very proud of that. It takes guys a while to get in there because I'm totally not used to getting fucked, but I'm starting to let guys with little cocks do it (God save me from the big ones).

So that's the story of my ass.

If you are reading this and thinking, "Why is he telling me this?" I would say that you are either very stupid or very fucked up.

All the Wrongs That
Have Been Done to Me

❧

So now I have to tell you about why I'm bitter and about all the wrongs that have been done to me and why I'm angry at the world.

My anger is not quite all consuming — not quite. I have to constantly keep it under control because it's always in danger of getting out of hand.

Like just about everyone else's anger, my anger is about the unjustness of the universe. In case you don't know, the universe is unjust, God is cruel, and life is unfair. If you haven't figured this out then you are either really young or you are living in some sort of deluded bubble that will burst eventually — don't worry, it will — when you get sick and/ or die.

The specifics of the wrongs done to me have to do with homophobia.

Sigh.

I started a gay theatre when I was 30 years old and just out of school. Originally it wasn't a gay theatre; it was just a theatre devoted to "theatrical poetry," but when I finally came out I made the theatre gay and started to write plays about gay poets.

At the time, I was living in the deluded bubble. My parents had, wrongly it turns out, convinced me that I could succeed in anything that I did and that I was so special and talented that the world would love me even if I came out. Of course they never said this to me — both of my parents really had to struggle with me being homosexual — and only my father has actually told me that he loves me despite my homosexuality. My mother died before she could say that, and I don't think she ever would have said it anyway. But my mother always made me think that I was special and that we had a very special arrangement. I thought that she could read my mind up until my mid-teens. Not literally, but I conducted my life as though my mother could read my mind, which means that if I actually wanted to do something bad (like be gay or say "fuck") I figured that she would somehow hear about it and so I would never do shit like that. Of course, she couldn't hear about it unless I told her, but I was so attached to her in a sick way that I thought she would just, well, know. My mother was the typical fucked up homo's mother who loves her son more than her husband and pretty well any man. She was obsessed with me and I still have to deal with all the false expectations of love and happiness that she set up for me, and made me expect from the world.

From my father I just got all this expectation that I would succeed, and in a lot of ways I have, superficially; I have a good job as a teacher and I am somewhat "famous" in the sense that a lot of people in Toronto know my name and know who I am. This makes my father very proud. I can understand that. But it's kind of a burden that he expects so much of me.

So one way or another I got the idea from my parents that I would be successful in my work, or that I had to be, or that it was inevitable. Of course I had my moments of doubt, and still do, but basically I think I am very talented, and always have thought so. And sure enough, the power of positive thinking actually does bring results. When I say that I'm very talented I actually am not being conceited because I don't think that's unusual. I think a lot of people are very talented, but the thing is that they don't toot their own horns. They have all sorts of voices (usual parental voices in their heads) telling them the opposite of what the voices in my head told me — that whatever they try they will fail at. I'm pretty convinced that it isn't my talent that has made me successful in my work, but instead the fact that I'm so fucking conceited and sure of myself. I succeeded because unlike most of the other really talented smart people in the world, I actually thought I was smart and talented and wasn't afraid of putting myself out there, in fact I craved it and needed it to survive.

I know you're thinking: "I thought he said he was a sad old faggot and now he's going on about being a success. Where does the sad old faggot part come in?"

Well, when I said I had high expectations, you weren't really cluing into what I meant. I have always thought I was branded for success, but in my mind, the success was not just that a few people in Toronto, Ontario, Canada would know my name. I imagined world domination.

I'm serious. Not in the sense of being a dictator, but in the sense that I would be famous — like Federico Fellini, or J. D. Salinger or somebody. I always figured that I would be a very famous writer or director or something, and that the world would be at my feet and I would be published in the *New Yorker* and my plays ravishingly reviewed by the *New York Times*. Nothing even remotely like this has ever happened and that both makes me unhappy and makes me feel life is unjust.

I don't mean to make light of this. I think the world *has* been unjust to me. And it isn't just that my expectations have been wildly unrealistic due to my parents. The fact is, I should be much more successful than I am, but I'm not, because of homophobia.

Well, first of all, I want you to think about me being a gay playwright and writing gay plays in Toronto from 1980 until now. Everybody thinks — wow, it must be great to be a gay playwright because most guys in the theatre are gay or gay positive and, after all, theatre is kind of a gay thing. It always has been, right? With men dressing up as women, and musicals and, well, just the damned expressiveness of it all — Oscar Wilde — the whole bit.

Well, *no*.

I'm saying no. I'm saying that the theatre is completely fucking homophobic, probably one of the most homophobic places in the world outside of sports. Just think about it. The problem is that in theatre, like in ballet, everyone thinks that if you're a man and you're involved then you are probably gay or bi or just swishy. It makes straight guys in theatre really mad — when they're trying to be like Al Pacino or Marlon Brando or James Dean — that people think they are fags. And as for the actual fags in theatre, they are either limp-wristed triple threats who think they can pass (no girlfriend, you can't) and that it's only someone like me who stops them from passing by bringing up the gay thing and being so outspoken, or they are full-blown closet cases, and me coming out totally threatens their cover. So because theatre is thought of as "gay" and there are lot of straight guys in it, and closeted gays, my presence as this big drag queen running a gay theatre actually makes a lot of people in theatre hate me. If I just shut up or died then theatre could go back to being about theatre, not about being gay.

But that's not why I'm bitter. That's just to give you an idea of the opposition I face. I'm bitter because, as I said, the fact is that I should be much more successful than I am. And I'm not successful partially because of homophobia in the theatre world, but also because of homophobia everywhere.

Think about it, I have produced more than 60 of my own plays since 1979 — basically because I've been able to do it, and because nobody else wants to, so I figured why not? I have received some rave reviews and audiences have, more often than not, been enthralled. I know it. I know it partially because they come up to me and tell me, or I watch them laughing. Whatever, I know that my work works.

The same thing with my novels.

I know that at least one or two of the seven of them is fucking good. I've received "You've changed my life" fan letters. Not from a lot of people. But from some people. And that means something when your publisher is so small that they can't spend any money on publicity to sell them.

What I'm saying is that basically there is a huge dispro-portion between my actual ability and the amount of success I receive. I will never break into the mainstream. Why? Because I write about gay stuff, gay men, gay relationships, gay sex. No one is interested, and it therefore can't be great art. That doesn't mean that when people pick up my plays by accident, or one of my books falls into their laps, they don't like them. But straight people would never think of reading them unless they were really avant-garde or open-minded.

Simply stated, I'm very talented and have a huge body of work and my work is smart and entertaining and sometimes even, I think, profound.

But no one could care less.

It's very hard to keep working when you realize you've reached the glass ceiling. When you realize fully that no matter how hard you try, no matter how excellent the work that you produce is, you can only go so far, and that "so far" is defined by people's tolerance for, well, two guys kissing.

Take this book for instance. I think it's going to be really great. I've just started writing it, so I can't be sure, and I've certainly been wrong before. It may end up in the garbage (my publisher may reject it). But the fact is that right now I think it's going to be fucking great, that it's going to be a one-of-a-kind book.

But that doesn't matter.

It will still get bad reviews. Especially from gay reviewers. The worst review I ever had was from Brett Josef Grubisic, some bitter old talentless faggot who was threatened by my gayness or my talent or God knows what. He totally ripped my last novel to shreds. Basically the problem is that I'll always just be the gay writer that gay writers hate because he's too gay and they are trying to assimilate. And lots of straight critics ignore my work because some of them are just scared of the whole gay thing. Especially the men. Women critics sometimes like my books, but straight men . . . Let's face it, there are very few of them who aren't worried that deep down somewhere they might be gay. And the straight men who are not worried about it have usually tried a little cock sucking and said something like "What's the big deal? It doesn't work for *me* anyway." Most other straight men are terrified they will become homosexuals if they get even the slightest taste of it. Judith Butler said that heterosexuality was fragile and it certainly is — straight men think their straightness may disappear at the flick of a towel. So straight male critics are not about to read my novels, much less give them good reviews. Instead the glowing raves go to gay novelists who manage *not* to talk about anything gay — guys like Alberto Manguel, or Colm Tóibín — which also ensures that gay novelists don't write a lot of gay stuff. . . .

And there's absolutely nothing I can do about all that.

A Horrible Thing That Happened to Me Recently That Makes Me Think My Life Is Almost Over

∽

Well, it is. I'm 62. The first horrible thing that happened was that I lost my best friend. He dumped me. And it came as a complete surprise to me, which really doesn't say much for my sensitivity.

I met Hugh when I was in my late 30s. I had had a kind of nervous breakdown, after which I realized that I had to develop more sensible personal relationships and try to settle down. Hugh was a young publicist who was kind of good-looking and very nice, but mostly just smart and funny. I thought: "I'm going to do myself a favour. I'm going to fall in love with someone who won't torture me, someone who will be a companion, someone who will be a sensible choice."

Okay, here's some advice. Never decide to start a relationship with someone because you think they are a sensible choice. It never works. Now on the one hand, most people make sensible choices in relationships. This means they marry someone whom they are not in love with, but who will make a good companion. Now that's fine for those of us who are not interesting, romantic, complex, intelligent, or tortured. Sensible normal people — most people — don't need to fall in love. And they don't want to. And that's just fine. They will say that they "love" their partner and probably do, but it's no wild passionate crazy tortured thing. So most people make the sensible choice. But they don't think of it that way — because they would never even think of *not* being sensible.

But there are those of us who get our ideas about romance from movies or novels, and we are very demanding (or think we are) and we aren't willing to settle for a companion. We want someone to fall in love with (whatever that means). And we do fall in love, and usually with people who are wildly inappropriate, emotionally unavailable, just plain nuts, or all three. But what happens is, after we spend a lot of time falling in love with assholes who treat us like shit, we suddenly have an epiphany and decide, "I need to make a sensible choice and go out with someone who won't hurt me. I won't be in love with the sensible choice and they won't be that fabulous. It will just be a nice, easy, sensible loving relationship."

It never works.

This is what happened to me in my relationship with Christopher Newton — the ex-artistic director of the Shaw Festival. He saw me as a sensible choice. Before he went out with me he had been mainly going out with down-on-their-luck aboriginal youths who were usually criminals with drinking problems. When he met me, he thought, "Well, here's a guy who has very little body hair, which really turns me on, and who has a drinking problem, which I also find attractive, but he's also very smart and creative, but not a criminal. Maybe he should be my sensible choice." I know all this because at one point Christopher told me that I was his "lawyer." And I asked him what that meant and he said, "You know, everyone has a lawyer, a sensible choice to go out with."

I was insulted. I don't think anyone actually wants to be told they are somebody's sensible choice. Anyway, our relationship didn't work out, partially because I was 30 years old and probably the furthest thing from a lawyer you could ever imagine. I'm actually quite proud to say I was a complete failure at being somebody's sensible choice.

And why doesn't the sensible choice tactic work? Because the people who want to make sensible choices, the people who would even think of such an idea, are permanently addicted to crazy choices. Besides, who wants to fuck a sensible choice?

But that didn't mean that I couldn't try and convince myself that I was attracted to Hugh. I mean I was attracted to him, in a non-urgent way. He was a man and kind of handsome. There was just no chemistry. But we had a lot of fun together, ate sandwiches late at night, gossiped . . . Anyway, we broke up, but then we moved on to the relationship I thought we were more suited for, which was to be "girlfriends."

Now the first thing you might notice about Hugh is that he is a publicist. In fact, when I met him, he was the publicist for my theatre company.

What does that say about me? That I would choose a publicist as my best friend? Not that there's anything wrong with publicists. But it's just very fucked up in a Judy Garland/Liza Minnelli type way. Is it possible that I am incapable of having a real friend — that I am, in fact, only capable of hanging around with someone who reflects back my wonderfulness to such an extent that he actually has the ability to write press releases about me? How can a relationship like that ever be equal or truly loving?

Hugh was a very good reflector. One of the things we had in common was discussing my "fame." He was very good at giving me advice about my career, the critics, and all that stuff. So he was part best friend, part personal publicist.

But I don't want you to think that I didn't value Hugh as a person, or that I didn't love him. What I loved about him most was that he was very caustic and droll; he really had a sense of humour about people. And like me, he loved women, but more because he loved divas and stars than anything.

We were friends for approximately 22 years.

Now during the last few years I did notice strange things happening between us. But I can't really say they were a signal for me that our friendship was in danger, even though probably they should have been.

And this is where it all gets really sad. I think it may have had to do with Hugh's partner. You see, Hugh — about five years after we broke up — met his long-term partner, Jim.

I had nothing against Jim, never did. I found him to be a really quiet person. And he was an advertising executive. And I didn't find him at all sexually attractive (but Hugh did tell me that he had a huge penis). Now I'm not one to judge people's relationships, and I had absolutely nothing against Jim, it's just that he's the furthest thing from what I would choose as a partner for myself. But that's fine, he wasn't my partner, he was Hugh's.

I was never quite sure what Jim thought of me. He was always very nice. But I just think ... well maybe I'm paranoid, but I think maybe Jim was, all along, not very pleased that Hugh was my friend.

Hugh and I loved to get drunk and gossip. And then at the end of the night he would get *so* drunk that I would have to ditch him. Now to be fair, I was usually on my way to the baths. But also, Hugh would just get to the point where he was starting to fall asleep on his feet. So then I knew it was time to go. And when I told him I was going, we would sometimes leave the bar arm in arm (me holding him up) and sure enough, he would say something on our way out of the bar like, "That's why I love you Sky, because you . . ." And then he would get very affectionate and hug me, which I liked. It was sweet as hell. But what was odd to me at the time — and I would only think of this at home, later, was — why did Hugh phrase his affection for me in that way? He would always say something like, "That's why I could never *not* be your friend," or, "That's the reason why I'll never leave you." And I remember thinking that the idea of *never* dumping me would only come into his head if the idea of dumping me *had*.

And it struck me a couple of times that the reason he said this was because he had to justify our relationship to Jim.

The other thing that was very sad and spooky — towards what I now know was the end of our friendship — was that I had to sort of force my way into Hugh's life because he just didn't have time for me. We wouldn't see each other for a couple of weeks and he would say, "I'm just so busy, and I can't go out, and I can't have a drink." So finally (and this is so fucking embarrassing to admit) I would say, "Well, if you can't go out, do you mind if I just come to your place and watch television with you? I mean if you and Jim are just sitting around watching TV, maybe I could join you?" And I did that. I literally did that. I would go over to their place at about eight o'clock to watch some TV series or special that we all liked, and drink booze and snack. What kills me is that at the time I had no idea how ridiculous this was. I was actually forcing myself into their family life. I mean, if you can, imagine sitting on the couch with your spouse watching your favorite movie and then having your best friend drop by and insert himself between the two of you and start munching popcorn.

Because that's pretty much what I was doing.

And then it all came crashing down. I was totally shocked — even though I suppose I shouldn't have been. I was doing a reading of a bunch of poems I wrote about my mother — *The Mommiad* — and in the collection there is a poem about my mother and I going for a drink at Alexander's, the old bar in Sutton Place, hoping to catch a glimpse of Liza Minnelli, who was staying there. In the poem there's a one-line joke where I say, "My friend claims he was there but to this day I don't think he was."

That line refers to Hugh.

So Hugh sends me an email the next day saying, "I can no longer be your friend. I can't be treated in this way. As if I do not exist. I was there on that day with your mother and the fact that you tried to wipe out my existence is just typical of our whole relationship. Please do not try to email me or call me. I will not answer. I can't take it anymore, being erased like this. Our friendship is over. I've had enough."

I was in a state of hurt shock. And the thing is, I really don't have anything to say about this except that maybe Hugh was right. I didn't mean to hurt his feelings, which is what I tried to tell him at the time. The point is that I should have known, should have been a better friend, should have been more sensitive to him and to all my other friends. But I wasn't and I'm not.

And ever since, I've been losing friends. I think one of the reasons is because I told too many of them about how Hugh had deserted me. That was a very stupid thing to do. I think a lot of them thought, "Wow, come to think of it, Sky *is* an insensitive bastard; I think I'll dump him too." Now most of my friends are alcoholics, like me, so it could just be that they're all getting old and life is starting to close in on them and they just don't want to be social anymore.

But hey, I guess I'm the last of a dying breed — the sociable alcoholic. I'm drunk as a skunk at least two nights a week but I still want friends.

But nobody wants me.

Something
Else Horrible

Then there was my hip replacement. It's one thing losing all your friends and it's another when you realize that you're not long for this world and that you could so easily die in a hospital because nobody cares.

I have arthritis and had to have my hip replaced — big deal. It's four days in the hospital and it was painful, but that that was nothing compared to the treatment by the nurses and the staff. Those days were sheer *hell*.

First of all, what were left of my friends came to visit me, which was nice. But it was a descent into hell for most of them too. I could tell that being there upset them as much as it did me — all they could think of was my mortality. But especially, also — theirs. They were just uncomfortable and incapable of giving. One person (I won't say who) broke down in tears and started complaining about how horrible her life was — because I guess my pain reminded her of her own disappointing existence. That wasn't very comforting. The only person who was really nice — that is, nice enough to listen to all my pain and woes — was Keith Cole. And he brought me a sub.

But the worst thing was the hospital itself — the staff and the neglect. First of all it was fucking hot in there. And of course you can't open up a window. What doofus — or was it an insane tormentor — came up with that system? I was in bed, hardly able to walk, and there was *nothing* I could do about the heat. It was very hard to sleep. All I could keep doing was asking the nurses for ice, which they would bring and treat me as if I was being oh so very selfish and demanding. And when I'd ask them about turning down the heat they'd say, "Oh yeah, it is a bit hot in here, sorry about that, there's not really much we can do." It was like Chinese water torture: "Oh yes, we're pulling your nails out slowly one by one. Sorry, I guess that must be a little uncomfortable — but that's the way it goes."

I had this completely nauseating little physiotherapist who made me feel 100 years old. I'll never forget him. He talked to me as if I was a potato or a piece of overcooked beef — really cheery and distant — and he was so fucking beautiful in a short, too-tanned, muscly, Latino sort of way. I could have killed him. And I had to have this catheter up my penis because I couldn't pee properly and my bladder was getting full, and this little dictator made me do a leg exercise on my second day. It really hurt to do the exercise. And I asked timidly, not wanting to rock his perfect boat, "Should I be doing this with a catheter in, cuz it kinda hurts?" because it was fucking agony. But he continued treating me the way you would treat any old potato or soufflé — "Oh no, don't worry about that" — very condescending. And then I went to sleep after the exercise and when I woke up there was blood coming out of my penis. You haven't lived until you've had blood coming out of your penis. Thank God a nurse finally agreed to take the damn catheter out.

But the rest of the nurses were monsters. The system there is terrible. There is a new nurse every six hours. Every nurse has her own temperament, routine, attitude about you, ideas about drugs, etc. And they don't communicate. I guess they write things down on their little clipboards, but whenever I tried to ask them questions about pills or my treatment, they didn't seem to know anything about my "case." I tried to get off the meds because they were making me sicker than the pain. I got the doctor to agree. But then one of the nurses saw I didn't take my pill and asked, "Why aren't you taking your pill?" (It was a heavy duty narcotic.) "Because the doctor said I didn't have to," I said. "But aren't you in pain?" she asked, irritated that I was not acting like every other patient. "The pain's not so bad and I don't want to take it," I said. She got very huffy. "Well that's a waste of a good pill," she said, sweeping it into the garbage, much more concerned about the pill than me.

I don't know if it's possible to fully express what it's like to be in pain and surrounded by people who are "just doing their jobs." I know this sounds intolerant and maybe classist of me, but I didn't meet any Florence Nightingales. I met a lot of nine-to-fivers who were pretty irritated by me and the job. They put up a kind of wall that said "Please don't bug me and don't ask any questions, and God knows don't ask for anything *extra*. My life is very stressed and I don't need the further stress of your being a needy argumentative patient."

And on top of it all they put me next to … not some nice feisty little old lady getting a new hip, who could have mothered me and told me cheery brave stories, but an odd, demented old British man who was obviously dying. How could anyone be dying in an arthritis hospital? I spent a lot of time listening as his horrific life wound down to nothing. He kept talking to his wife, Myrtle, when she wasn't there, and he'd call the nurses in and say with his British accent: "I'm going to get that article down to the head office, could you kindly send it off for me?" I guess he used to be a journalist. And the nurses — most of whom barely spoke English — would say "Pardon?" and then, realizing he was demented, "I'll do what I can, sir." And his family would come and visit him, and they were all upper class British white people with names like Reginald and Jasper. Because of the curtain separating us I could only hear their voices and watch the shuffling of their white deck shoes. They'd ask the nurses, "Is he walking on his operated leg?" They were trying to act concerned but they weren't. But of course he wasn't exercising, he was just lying in bed, dying and moaning and talking to his dead wife.

It was a nightmare.

The catheter incident and my general treatment by the nurses — as well as the demented dying man beside me — just made me realize how easy it would be to die in a hospital and have no one really care.

And generally as I get older I just realize that doctors give up on you. That's the way it is. You're old and they just figure … "Why Bother?" (To quote Bette Midler *again*.) They think you'll die of old age anyway before you die of anything you're actually suffering from, and they think you should be grateful for that. I mean I understand, I get it, I wouldn't want to help old people either, even if it *was* my job.

But if you wonder why old granny doesn't want to go to the hospital, maybe this is the reason.

My Boyfriend

~

I'm not going to talk about him. You're wondering, how can Sky Gilbert write a book about himself and not talk about his partner? I can't talk about him because he would kill me. And rightfully so. I think he has a very good argument. He points to famous men whose wives have managed to remain incognito. When Stéphane Dion was cabinet minister, my partner would always point out Dion's wife, Janine Kreiber. I bet you didn't even know her name. If you Wikipedia her this is what it says: "Janine Kreiber is a Canadian political scientist, studying terrorism and international security. Her husband is Stéphane Dion, former leader of the Liberal Party of Canada." That's it. There doesn't seem to be anything else. My partner (I don't even want to tell you his name) says that's the way it should be. If somebody is famous and their partner does not wish to be famous, then the partner's privacy should be respected.

Okay, I get it. But how are you supposed to understand anything about me if I don't talk about him? I'm going to tell you about everything else so what about if we make a deal and just say that whatever seems to be missing . . . is him.

If there's a hole in this, an emptiness at the centre, it is filled up by him.

Now I feel guilty.

I feel I should stop writing this stupid book because how can it be real if I don't talk about him?

But can't you see that the realness of our relationship is proved by the fact that I can't actually talk about him? I could only talk about him if I was faking it.

Honestly.

I can't imagine life without him. He's a soul mate. People say that all the time, but what does it really mean? It means somebody who shares your sense of humour and particular view of the world. On the essential things, my partner and I agree, completely, and I don't think I could ever find anyone who would ever agree with me as much as he does.

On the unessential things though, we have a lot of arguments.

See if this makes sense. I am completely certain that my boyfriend is and will be an essential part of my life forever, so much so that I cannot even imagine discussing him as being a problem, or causing problems, or whatever. I mean of course we have problems but . . . we work them out. I know what I get from him is unconditional love, which, I realize, is a big deal.

Okay, let me put it this way. I have lots of friends who

say, "Oh you're so lucky ... you have a boyfriend." This is just like my mother, who always used to say, "You're so lucky, you have friends."

First of all I am *not* fucking lucky. Having friends and a boyfriend isn't a matter of luck. It's a matter of hard work (and I haven't been working hard enough on my friends, which is probably why they're all leaving my life like rats leave a sinking ship). Second of all, having a boyfriend doesn't solve anything or make anything easier. Sure, it fills a giant hole in your life, but there's still a lot of other stuff to deal with.

If this seems crazy to you, if you're thinking either "how can he be unhappy if he has a boyfriend who loves him unconditionally?" or "if he really loved his boyfriend then he wouldn't have any problems," then I would suggest that your idea of relationships is deluded and involves codependence. And you are expecting all your problems to be solved by your lover, or husband, or whoever they are. And that's just nuts.

My Sad Sex Life

~∂

My sex life has always been focused on my promiscuous activities. In other words, I'm a big slut. Maybe if I described to you my latest three sexual encounters, you could make your own judgements about how sad and fucked up this senior's sex life really is.

Okay, the best sex I recently had was when I got picked up by this guy at my favorite bar, Woody's.

Most, in fact *all*, of my best sexual encounters recently involve people who call me "Daddy." I'm not exactly sure what this means. Of course it means that they are attracted to me because I'm older, which is great. But it could also mean that they are actually fantasizing that I am their father, or they are comparing me to their own fathers, who they want to have sex with. Now if this is true I don't really want to know. The main thing is that they are attracted to old guys (yay, old guys!) and that this is a good thing for me, because I'm not very good at having sex with people who are not attracted to me. That may seem like an obvious thing to say but I don't think so. A lot of people *do* have sex with people who are not attracted to them. For instance often husbands and wives have sex with their partners just out of obligation. Or husbands have sex with hookers, which is basically paying someone to pretend to be attracted to you. Neither of those situations turns me on. I have to absolutely believe that I am the hottest thing since sliced bread for whomever I'm having sex with. As I get older, this can get tougher, but then again, I always have the "Daddy" thing to fall back on.

The Woody's guy definitely had a Daddy obsession. When I first saw him I didn't pay much attention to him. I was standing out on the patio talking to somebody else and I happened to notice him. Tall, slender, hipsterish, glasses, trendy skinny jeans, beard — the whole shemozzle. I might have glanced at him. Then I went back inside. About half an hour later I was taking a piss (very drunk) when he broke into the cubicle. I guess I leave the door open when I'm pissing at gay bars hoping against hope that something like this will happen. So the door was probably ajar or unlocked. Anyway, he pushes his way in, curls down on the floor next to the toilet and says, "Oh Daddy, please do anything you want to me, Daddy." So I stuck my dick in his mouth. (Wouldn't you? He was very cute.)

As I say, I'm not that into getting blow jobs. But I was drunk and my limp dick rolling around in his mouth seemed to make him happy. And he was very into keeping up the running dialogue, or monologue, which I found extremely sexy. (Dirty talk only works when you're attracted to them.) So then he started saying things: "Oh I want to taste you everywhere, Daddy, I want to lick you all over, Daddy," which again, was fine with me. So I let him do some tasting and licking, and he seemed to really like it under my armpits. This was really turning me on. So I said, "Let's go someplace else" and he was like a happy puppy dog following me around. I thought we could go over to the Eagle, which has a backroom. Then I could come all over him. Anyway, that was my plan. I knew he would be into it. He was like "Sure, Daddy" so we left the bar and went a few doors down to the Eagle. I led him up to the toilet, which I thought would be more private than the Eagle backroom. So we're going crazy at it there. I'm sucking him and he's sucking me, and he has a really nice big pierced dick, as those confirmed bottoms sometimes do. After we had been there for about 15 minutes — and the bar was practically empty, I swear — some idiot bartender bangs on the door (which we couldn't close completely, but we tried to close it, honest) and he says, "Take that someplace else." Or something to that fucking effect. Jesus.

Where were we supposed to go? I wanted some sort of privacy. It was a sad old Thursday night and nobody was in the goddamn bar except for us, and it was the toilet in a leather bar next to the backroom where fags go to have public sex. Who could we possibly be bothering with our Boy Loves Daddy antics? Hey, that spoiled the buzz. And besides, I was tired and old and I knew I wasn't going to come. So I dragged my hipster acolyte out on the patio where a couple of guys were having a smoke. They didn't pay any attention to us — which was good because My Little Daddy's Boy was curled up around my leg like a dog, panting and gazing up at me and begging for more action. I pulled him to his feet and planted a big wet affectionate kiss on his thick very kissable lips and said something I hoped would sound like Humphrey Bogart in *Casablanca*, something like — "See ya later, kid." I mean it's true that the problems of a couple of little people don't matter a hill of beans in this crazy world, but they mattered enough for *this* dumb barkeep to stop me from coming on my Boy Toy's lean sweet chest. (To be fair, it probably wasn't the barkeep's fault and he probably wasn't being dumb. The police are always cracking down on gay Toronto backroom bars.)

The second story takes place at the baths and is just as crazy. This guy was perfect — an absolutely perfect match for me. I was sitting in my room on the bed watching porn and this young good-looking guy stopped at the door. He was dressed in a full very stylish suit and carrying a briefcase. Now for you to understand this story, you have to understand something about the way the gay bathhouse works. Most guys walk around naked or semi-naked. So if somebody is standing in front of your door looking in and they are fully clothed and carrying a briefcase no less, then you know that we're talking about a commitment. Not a lifetime commitment, of course, but long enough for him to take off his clothes. And he has to lay them out on the bed or floor or whatever, and then of course when the sex is over he's going to at least collect all his clothes, if not put them all back on again. These things take time, right? So the sex had better be good, or at least you'd better let him stay long enough to make it seem worthwhile for him to gather up all his clothes again. Many a time I've let some drunken numbnut into my room only to have it turn out after the first couple of minutes that I realize I can't possibly have sex with him — he's ugly or smelly or mean or just too drunk or whatever — at which point he wants to kill me, and seriously doesn't want to leave or won't. So I know that if there's a guy who's fully clothed with a briefcase at my door then I'd better be pretty sure I want to have sex with him for a substantial amount of time if I let him in.

This guy — well I just let him in, I didn't even think about it.

So in he comes and pretty well leaps on the bed and it's all about lying down with me and kissing.

All very romantic kissy face. This guy was really into it and so was I. So we're kissing and kissing and kissing and looking into each other's eyes and kissing and touching each other's faces and jerking off and rubbing and gazing into each other's eyes and some more deep kisses, wet kisses, full-mouth tongue exploring, it just goes on and on. And he's very polymorphously perverse. By this I mean he is not very goal oriented in his lovemaking. He just seems to want to roll all over each other. But this suits me fine. I mean did he read a manual on how to make love to an older man? It sure doesn't matter if my dick is hard or not, all that matters is us tasting and touching every inch of each other. And I roll him over and lick his ass for what seems like hours and then he does the same for me. Who's the top here? Nobody cares, thank God. Anyway this went on for what seemed like an eternity until I finally came because I was just so tired I couldn't hack it anymore. And when he left I had lots of time to gaze at his full buttocks and hairy legs and lazy, easy devil-may-care mannerisms.

The third example? That's the bad fuck. He's at the baths too. He's another total Daddy obsessive. A regular. I can't get rid of him, couldn't get rid of him if I tried. I always say that I'll never have sex with him again, just because I think he's high on something and the sex with him has gotten particularly boring recently, but I don't think there's anything I can do. A bad fuck that's somehow good is in like a dirty shirt, you just can't stop returning to the scene of the crime.

He's another kisser and he likes gazing into my eyes in a dumb, adoring way. He also loves mirrors, and there is always one in the room at the bathhouse I go to.

Anyway, let me describe him, so you get the picture. He's very twink — I don't know, in his 20s somewhere — blond shaved head, angelic expression. He has a slender but not very toned body, a quite large dick with a huge head on it, and a lovely round ass with blond furry fuzz on it. That seals the deal. I just could bury my nose in that ass for hours and I love it and he knows it. He likes to sit on my face, then turn on the lights in the room and bounce around on it, looking the mirror. He calls me Daddy a lot and I've done all the requisite Daddy shit, like spanking him and force feeding him my cock and I think I've actually fucked him a couple of times. I don't know. Honestly, I was too drunk to remember.

But he's relentless. By that I mean that he just won't not have sex with me even if I'm tired and limp and out of it, and not turned on. He just has to get that fucking photograph of the two of us that he takes in his head every time he looks at himself sitting on my lap in the mirror.

Lately he's also been inviting people into my room, which is okay, especially because he completely keeps up this fiction that we are lovers or fuck buddies and the other person is an interloper. He looks at me like . . . "Daddy, should we do this one?" And sometimes Daddy says yes and sometimes no . . . depending on my mood. And the other person is usually more into him than me, but totally buys the fact that we are some sort of weird gay swinger couple, which we are not.

I've seen this boy lots of times in the bars with his twink boyfriends, but he kind of won't acknowledge me, or if he does it's with great embarrassment. Maybe he's ashamed of his Daddy fetish? I don't care.

And that's the basis of all this. It's fun but I don't care and I'm actually beginning to wonder, what's the point? I don't mean to sound like Dr. David Reuben, M.D. (Remember him, the sex doctor?) But what's the point of all this meaningless sex?

Fun, of course — that's the point. And it is fun sometimes. But sometimes I just think I'm getting too old to really enjoy it, especially when I end up with Daddy Baths Twink Boy riding my face and I can't get hard or come, and it's four o'clock in the morning, and he can't get enough of looking at himself in the mirror, and he won't go away.

The Street They Haven't
Named After Me Yet

༄

Things seem to be coming to a head and I'm not making a fucking sexual joke.

I'm just saying that there has to be some climax, some endgame, to all this being a sad old faggot business. And I don't mean death (or I don't want to mean it). Should I just slow down? I know I don't want to. I make fun of the gardening fags, the fags who started being old when they were 40, and embraced old age and started gardening, and how now and then they might sit up, take their eyes off the ground and gaze up at some cute young thing, thinking "There he goes . . . that fine young man . . . with that firm young ass . . . ah well, those days are past."

Well, I just don't think I could be that person.

But is there something between planting petunias and letting that firm young ass ride your face when you're drunk and nearly being suffocated at four in the morning?

I'm not sure, but I've decided to try a few things that might instigate a little change in my life. Turn things around.

It all seemed like a direct route to depression and/or death. Couldn't I find a detour? I should be honest, though. It wasn't just a sudden revelation; it didn't just occur to me that my life was a bit too sad for words. It all started when somebody said they were going to name a street after me. *Maybe.*

Can you think of anything more frustrating?

Brendan Healy, present artistic director of the theatre that I used to run, emailed me and said, "A neighbourhood group near Buddies in Bad Times Theatre is renaming the laneway next to the theatre. And we suggested they name it after you. We would have to know that you gave us permission."

"Why sure," I said.

Of course they could have my permission. Of course the city of Toronto could name a fucking street after me. Why not? I really thought I deserved it.

And then I started to tell people and they were very impressed. Like my barber. I live in the small city of Hamilton, just outside of Toronto, and I decided to tell my barber, who is a really nice guy. He went ballistic. "A street? Are you serious? They are naming a street after you?"

"Well, they might be," I said shyly, having let the cat out of the bag.

"Well, I knew you were a somewhat famous guy but I had no idea."

There was a guy sitting in the barbershop and he overheard our conversation. "Oh didn't you know that guy whose hair you are cutting is famous? He's very famous in Toronto," he said.

"Oh yeah, really famous?" asked my barber.

"Oh yeah, he's a big deal. You are cutting Sky Gilbert's hair."

"Gee, I didn't know you were such a big deal, Sky," said my barber. I know that Hamilton Tiger-Cats players get their hair cut there, and I felt that in my barber's eyes I had suddenly joined the ranks.

But nothing could compare to my father's reaction, which was beyond over-the-top. I thought he was going to shit his pants. "I can't believe it. That is amazing. I'm so proud of you." And of course he immediately — as soon as he hung up — called all the relatives. "I'm going to tell everyone," he said. And I'm sure he did.

Now every time I call him the first thing he says to me is, "So any news on *The Street?* I mean I can't get over it, Sky, I really can't." I always have to interrupt him — "No, Dad, I told you, it may take a while for them to make a decision. And who knows, they may veto naming it after me. There are some people who don't like me, you know."

"Well, keep me posted, will you?"

Of course I promise to keep him posted but I know that he's just going to drive me crazy about it and that he's much more excited than he should be.

Then I begin to think, why did I tell him? Especially when it wasn't for sure yet?

I told him so he would be proud of me.

Or maybe because I'm the proud one.

Maybe, in fact, this means a lot to me because . . . Because there's not that much going on in my life. Because I'm so desperate for something to live for, some sort of recognition.

Because I'm actually a little obsessed about the idea that somebody might name a street after me.

Discovering I am obsessed with this upset me.

Why?

Think about it. Who gets streets named after them?

Dead people, that's who.

Then There Was
the Awful Night

∾

Then there was the awful night.

I did something very embarrassing that made me realize I'm totally fucked up.

Though I'm sure that's evident to you by now.

It was the beginning of several awful misguided incidents, but this was the first.

So there's this young actor whom I have worked with several times. He is extremely beautiful. I don't know how to describe him except to say that. If I say that he's tall and blond and well muscled — well aren't there *so* many men like that? But then he has a perfect face, which is a killer for me. Very high cheekbones, thick straight lips, all angles, eyes with a slight feminine catlike slant to them, full blond straight hair. I cast him in a play that was directed by someone else at this summer theatre, and I spent the whole summer falling in love with him. Except I didn't.

How do I explain this? Well, of course I know that Nathaniel would never be interested in me sexually. He is on the cusp of ... What? Of everything, for Christ's sake. And I'm on the cusp of nothing. Literally. Anyway. I know that Nathaniel would never want to touch me. Or at least I thought I thought that. So when I was watching rehearsal of my play, I would just gaze at his thick furred thighs. In case you haven't guessed, I have a weakness for thick furry thighs in cut-off shorts, basically because they are attached to thick furry asses. He used to wear cut-off shorts to rehearsal, and it was very hard for me to remember that he wasn't wearing them for my benefit. The thing about cut-offs is you're always waiting for an errant dick or a ball to fall out of them. That never happened but ... oh God, he drove me crazy. And we would get drunk together and have these long talks that were very intense but funny, you know, because Nathaniel is very campy and self-deprecating. Of course he thinks he's worthless and has nothing but lousy boyfriends who treat him like shit. Of course. That's the way perfect guys always are. Everyone always thinks that perfect guys are conceited but most of them — even though they may know that people think they are hot — have no idea of their own self-worth. And yeah, so they get treated badly. Nathaniel always had a funny sad sob story to tell me about some hot guy who had mistreated him.

And I worried about him. I worried about him very much. In a fatherly way. Or maybe a grandfatherly way — he was like 35 years younger than me.

I have to admit that when I met Nathaniel, I was thinking about Larry Clemson.

I fell in love with Larry Clemson when I first came out.

He was again tall and blond, very pretty, and effeminate, and he had no idea of his self-worth. When I first came out I was in a "bisexual support group," which was basically a place for guys who were coming out to get preyed upon by older men. There was a guy who was after me in the group. His name was Spencer. He was absolutely completely unattractive to me — thin and hairy and just extremely effeminate in that way that he sounded like a gay character on a TV show. Of course he would have done anything to get me alone. (I think I actually gave in once and slept with him.) And Larry was being chased by Liam, the guy who ran the group, who was this 50ish university professor with a big belly and a bald head. Well, I was in love with Larry from the moment I met him because I was just coming out of the closet and he was sweet and beautiful. But who did Larry sleep with? Not me. Liam. I was really pissed off and shocked. I know it was just because Liam was fucking persistent and wouldn't let Larry alone until he fucked him.

This is for those of you who can't get laid. I don't know if you're aware of this, but the reason any old ugly guy can get laid is simply because they are persistent. I remember I was staying at a house once with a man who was the ugliest man on earth. This was when I was working at Niagara-on-the-Lake, and when I was lonely, before I started fucking Christopher Newton. How shall I describe him? Basically he had a face like a hatchet and an ugly flabby body and (as I was to find out) a tiny penis. And I didn't even *like* him. But we were spending the night in the same room together, and we stayed up all night talking because he insisted on it. And then he wouldn't let me go to sleep until I let him suck me off. And you know I finally decided, okay go ahead, suck me off, I don't give a fuck, if it will shut you up, then okay. I think more people than you might know have sex with people just to shut them up and make them go away.

Well, Liam, who ran the group, was like this. I asked him once what his secret was for getting laid. (I wanted to ask him about Larry Clemson but was afraid to actually do it.) And he said, "You have to proposition seven guys in one night. If you can't get laid by the seventh guy, then give up." Seven guys. Can you believe it? I can barely come on to one — I get all angsty and tortured and I usually have to be drunk, which means that I'm even less appealing than usual. (I always have to be approached by someone; I never approach.) So Larry was just one of the seven guys Liam approached one night. But with Larry he got lucky. And he probably got lucky because Larry could feel that Liam didn't really care ... because he was going to ask another six guys anyway, so there was no pressure. But also Larry probably gave in because he just wanted Liam to shut the fuck up.

Well, anyway, beautiful Larry and I did have one perfect time together; we went to Provincetown and we were sluts. He didn't have any luck getting laid but I met a really cute waiter named Dominic, who was all over me. This made me feel better after I had to watch Larry sleeping with Liam in our "bisexual" group. (Had any of the men in the bisexual group besides me *ever* had sex with a woman?) But it wasn't just schadenfreude, I really enjoyed going on vacation with Larry, and we became close friends.

Well, after we went to Provincetown, Larry met a guy from New York City. This was back in 1982. And what happened? You guessed it. Larry got AIDS and died. Just like that. It was incredibly sad. Larry's boyfriend was Latino. He met Larry in Toronto but took him to New York. Then he broke up with him, and Larry really dove into Latino and black culture. Larry told me that he would go to all these black and Latino bars and he would be the only white guy in the room. Well, you can imagine. Larry being the only white guy in the room — and being perfect, a perfect pale flower — he opened up for all these men and got banged to death, literally. This was before AIDS was a chronic illness. This was when it could kill you just like that.

I remember Larry phoned me from New York City and basically told me, "I've got it, the big 'A'."

I said, "Oh no, I can't believe it, you know can't they do anything?" I mean what the hell can you say? He said no and that basically he was going to die and hung up. It was horrible.

So Larry comes up when I think about Nathaniel. It's not that I think he's going to die of AIDS — they have all sorts of drugs to deal with that now. It's just that when someone is that beautiful and sweet and vulnerable, they are bound to come to a bad end. They will either get fucked around by men who only want them for their looks, or they will just — for sure — get old and stop being beautiful, when their whole existence revolves around that beauty.

So anyway, Nathaniel was in a show, and I went to see it because I was thinking of casting him in another one of my plays. He was playing Hedwig in *Hedwig and the Angry Inch*. Don't get me started about this stupid play. I had never seen it — I think I saw a bit of the movie and didn't much like it. But because Nathaniel was starring in it I was kind of duty-bound to go and watch the whole damn thing.

It was an awful event. At the time I had just directed a

play in Toronto that no one had gone to see, and everyone was going to see *Hedwig and the Angry Inch*. It was at a theatre called the Lower Ossington Theatre, which is, well, it's an awful place. It's the kind of theatre Toronto deserves these days because it's a piece of shit semi-amateur house for triple threats (actor-singer-dancers who have just graduated from the Randolph Academy for the Performing Arts) to strut their stuff. Toronto has recently become so fucking bourgeois because of all the condos, and basically all the people who live there now are stupid rich suburban people. This is why I don't live in Toronto. But anyway, these stupid people just want fucking pap; they want to go to a nice restaurant and all they require of the theatre is that the play not offend them, and not offend their date, so they can fuck their date afterwards. So what's very popular right now at the Lower Ossington Theatre are bad musicals like *Rent* and plays called things like "The Dinner Party," or "Engendering Tapas," or some other culinary name, and these plays are all about sexy people who have dinner parties where couples switch partners. Of course the people who come to see these shows would never play partner-switch. But they love to go to plays about that, because it makes them horny.

The same thing is true of *Rent*, which is a piece of shit play that — like *The Rocky Horror Show* — was also written to make straight people horny. But at least *Rocky Horror* is honest about that. *Rent* is one of those four-hanky crier plays that you go to so you can see the poor drag queen called Angel die. But actually it's a good thing that the drag queen dies, because that's what drag queens are supposed to do, get AIDS. Because after all, they are just too gay for this world, *and the audience*. And if they stayed onstage for too long you might have to hear the details of their actual fucking lives, which scares the hell out of audiences who are only into watching them be tragic figures who suddenly disappear.

Hedwig is not a play; it is a series of songs for a trans person who has had a botched sex-change operation.

Oh my God — have you ever heard of such a thing as a botched sex-change operation? I know lots and lots of trans people and I have never heard of such a thing. And Hedwig, who actually comes off as a gay man or a drag queen and not a transgender person at all, only gets the sex change so that she can get out of Berlin. So she doesn't really want to be a woman, she just does it for convenience. And instead of having his penis removed and a vagina put in, Hedwig ends up with this tiny little penis bump in the front. And the climax of the musical — get this — the stirring angry political moment, is when Hedwig's white trash closeted straight-acting boyfriend refuses to deal with her "front," her botched sex change. And Hedwig has this big trans lib moment that is like, "deal with my front — you have to deal with it." And all I can say is . . . Why? Why does he have to deal with it? Why should anyone be forced to find someone who is the victim of a botched sex-change operation attractive? Can you explain that to me? This isn't even about having sex with someone who is a trans person, it's about having sex with someone who has been the victim of a tragic disfiguring accident. But why should anyone be required to sleep with someone like that? It would be like saying, "You have to be open-minded and kind and loving and have sex with an amputee, and if you don't you are an awful person." Well, who says so?

I mean I'm all for differently abled people having all the sex they want to and in fact I'm sure a lot of them do. I've been very attracted to a number of dwarfs in my time. Dwarfs always turn me on because they look like they would have big hairy bums and big dicks on their small bodies (surprise!). And there are a couple of wheelchair guys I've seen who are totally cute and I would love to suck them off. In fact it's probably them who would reject me, cuz I am after all the *old guy*. But I don't think it's right that anybody should force somebody to have sex with them just because they've got some sort of disability.

Anyway, it's a stupid play, bad sex jokes, no real plot, and lousy songs except for the last song — but, listen to me, one song does not a musical make.

So there I was in this audience of hipsters and inappropriately dressed gay men. The seating was at tables and they sat me with a bunch of Asian women who didn't speak English. I felt completely out of place so the only thing I knew to do was get drunk. I was wearing a T-shirt and ripped jeans, which I thought was appropriate for a Friday night on the town, but all the fags in the room were all dressed up with sparkly shirts and bow ties. Lower Ossington Theatre is a tiny little dump of a theatre but it *does* have a bar.

So I suffered through the whole hour and a half of bad songs, and no plot or characters, and stupid blow job jokes. (I like a blow job joke as much as the next guy, but they have to be funny.) Nathaniel was heroic, so beautiful in his blond wig, and doing everything to entertain an audience who just basically didn't want to be upset by anything, but still wanted to feel that they were doing something "hip" by going to the theatre. When it was over I was quite drunk and waited for Nathaniel to come and talk to me because he had gotten me the free ticket. He had to meet all his fans of course, and particularly a fascistic faggot musical director (or was he the actual director?) who was giving him advice because he had a cold. "Go to bed early and wrap up your throat and make sure to drink some tea, and don't talk all night." Yeah, what-ever. I would have killed the guy, but Nathaniel was very nice. He was always very nice.

It was good that I was drunk because I could ignore Nathaniel's beauty. But I noticed that he was looking at me with a kind of concern that was strange and I wasn't sure what was going on. He pulled me away from the bar into a corner and said: "I have to talk to you about something. Do you mind if we meet somewhere and talk? The thing is, it has to be private."

I didn't know what to say. But I said: "Is something wrong?"

"No," he said. "I just need some advice, but it would be great if it could *not* be" — he smiled winningly — "where a lot of other people are around."

I asked him if he wanted to come over to my place for tea sometime. I don't drink tea, but I thought it sounded really innocent to invite him over for tea.

The whole thing was already making me nervous.

We worked out the whole thing via email and we decided that he was going to come over to my house the following Sunday night, after his Sunday matinee. The whole thing was crazy, but knowing he was coming over to visit was making me feel odd and . . . what? Romantic? Horny? I put it down to the Larry Clemson similarity at the time.

I should probably explain that I have never, never in my entire life, come on to someone that I've worked with. I've directed lots of cute actors. I fell in love with one once, but I was very sure not to come on to him until after the play was over. And yes, I put one of my ex-boyfriends in a couple of movies I made, but that was after we broke up. I completely believe that it will totally wreck a working relationship if there is some sort of hanky-panky going on. And on top of that, as someone who directs and casts actors I am extra sensitive to using my "power" — because I know it is one — for ill-gotten kisses. Above all I did not want to exploit anyone. And on top of that, I'm not attracted to guys who aren't attracted to me, so why would I want to force myself on some actor, anyway?

I knew that I was a mentor to Nathaniel, somebody he looked up to. He had struggled with coming out as an actor, for a while he had been in the closet and then he had come out in a big way, and joined this "gay idol" singing contest. For a while he had a shaved head and he had gained some weight — and it looked good on him, just like everything looked good on him — and it had been his big time to be an "out" gay actor. Then I had cast him in a gay play and now he was bravely doing gay parts — so I supposed that he saw me as someone who had kind of encouraged him to be more honest about who he was.

I knew all this, and there's no way — knowing that I was having Larry Clemsonish feelings about him — that I should have had a drink before he came over. That was absolutely the wrong thing to do. In fact, I had more than one or two; I had quite a few. Now anybody who knows me knows that when I drink it's completely invisible, nobody knows I'm drunk. But that doesn't mean that I don't do things that I shouldn't.

My boyfriend and I have a little apartment in Toronto, even though we have a house in Hamilton. Now we also have a deal that we're not supposed to fuck other people there. Which we don't. But we are allowed to have friends over. The only problem with having friends over is that it's a real flop-house, just basically a couple of twin beds and a chair and a TV. It's not even a real apartment. It kind of looks like a crack house (which is on purpose, because we don't live in Toronto, and we don't want to get too comfortable there, and when we stay in the apartment it's just to go out and have fun).

So I had to explain to Nathaniel that the apartment was always a bit of a shock to people. I mean I hardly ever have anyone over, but once in a while someone sees it and they're like, "Sky Gilbert lives here?" meaning "this dump?" And I have to explain that I don't, that it's just a "pied à terre," etc. Anyway, so I thought he was prepared. But nobody ever is.

I'd had three double vodkas, which is just the start of a usual night's drinking for me. I opened the door.

Of course he looked gorgeous. He always wears these loose flowing V-necked cotton shirts that kind of gently fall on his body so you can see the outline of everything underneath. Nathaniel is so beautiful that he really doesn't ever look as if he has tried to look that way. The other thing that was very much on my mind after six vodkas was his dick.

I couldn't stop thinking about Nathaniel's dick.

I had seen it because during the new being an "out" actor phase of his development, he'd played Wolf in *Bent*. Wolf is basically called that because he is actually hung like some large animal. This is the only stage direction I have ever read in a play that actually calls for an actor with a large penis. (Hmm. I wonder how you audition somebody for a part like that?)

And Nathaniel fit the bill. I actually had no idea that Nathaniel was playing Wolf when I went to see the play, I just knew that he was in *Bent* and I thought maybe he was one of the guys who has sex with another guy without touching him in the concentration camp (that's basically what happens in *Bent*, and it's actually a pretty good play). But no, it turns out that of course Nathaniel was playing the trick named Wolf, who one of the gay guys picks up before he goes to the concentration camp.

Wolf only has a few lines in one scene, but basically he's required to make his entrance from the bedroom naked.

Well, I didn't know which character Nathaniel was playing, honest, so imagine my surprise when he leapt onstage from stage left, his dick swinging. And what a dick it was. Hefty and long, it must have been nine or ten inches. And I think it was semi-erect, partially because it's hard to imagine a limp dick being so big, and partially because I was watching his dick very carefully in the totally naked scene he had after his entrance and I noticed that it got a little smaller (not much though). This means that he must have been jerking himself off to make it semi-hard before his entrance.

When he came out it was very funny because there were a lot of old ladies in the audience (there always are, for mainstream theatre) and a couple of them actually gasped when his dick turned up. I heard one of them say, "Oh no" and another one say, "Oh my God." They were very frightened. I hope I never get so old that a big dick frightens me. It was like they were saying, "There's no need for someone to have a dick like that." After the show I congratulated Nathaniel on his performance but it was very awkward because everything I said seemed to refer to largeness or fabulousness. "It was a great show," I said, and suddenly thought that maybe he thought I was referring to him showing off his dick.

Well, after seeing that dick I just never felt the same about Nathaniel. It was just so hard to believe that on top of being so tenderly beautiful and sweet, he was also hung like a horse. And I must say, that is my favourite turn-on — a pretty face and a big dick. The whole idea of someone having this gorgeous boyish sweetness attached to a big man handle just drives me crazy. That's why I love sweet looking boys with hairy legs. It's like they are satyrs underneath their clothes.

So having Nathaniel into our little crack apartment, the kind of apartment that looks like it was made to fuck or do drugs in (even though that's not what we do there, honest) put a kind of weird pressure on the meeting.

So when Nathaniel came in, all this was on my mind.

He was very sweet and polite as always. I sat Nathaniel in the only chair, and I sat on the bed. We had a little tea and made small talk. And because there was no table, Nathaniel had to put his tea on the floor, which made me feel that the apartment was very obviously uncivilized. Kind of savage, actually (tea on the floor?). But then Nathaniel said that he wanted to stand up and talk to me.

It was all very weird. I stood up opposite him and Nathaniel said, all self deprecating, as was his way, "I'm really worried about this and you're the only person that I could talk to about it because I admire you so much and you know, you helped me come out as an actor." I thanked him for the compliment. Then he said that what he had to say was really stupid and he was ashamed to ask me the question. I told him not to be ashamed. He said that he couldn't help it. Then he reminded me again about how he had gone through this period of trying to strip himself of all his gay mannerisms when he was trying to get straight parts and now it was very difficult for him to act, because he had been reading a lot of David Mamet, and this was making him paranoid. I immediately knew what he was talking about.

David Mamet is a very talented American playwright. He can be very witty. (Except for his crazy lousy play *Edmond*. It's about a guy who goes into the depths of despair and ends up doing drugs and going with hookers. It's very uptight, melodramatic, moralistic, and Victorian. So if you really want to know how fucked up Mamet is, read that play.) Anyway, in his old age Mamet has turned into a kind of curmudgeon. He wrote a lot of really bad books about what theatre is and what art is, etc. His books are now pronouncements from on high. It's like, "I'm old. I've done so much and I'm so talented, so you have to listen to me because everything I say is right." Jesus. If I ever turn out like that, shoot me. (Hasn't David Mamet ever read "Ozymandias" by Shelley? "Look on my works ye mighty and despair. Nothing around remains . . .") David Mamet really thinks he has left a legacy. Let me tell you there is no legacy. When you're dead you're dead, it's over, get used to it. Don't get me started about fucking David Mamet.

Anyway, Nathaniel had made the mistake of reading David Mamet's *True and False* — which makes all these bullshit pronouncements about acting. In the book Mamet says, for instance, that you don't need to play a character, and should never do that, because playing a character is lying. Bullshit. That's all acting is: putting on a character. But for Mamet it's like, "just be yourself and say the lines and you will BE the character." Oh yeah, right. If you want to get an idea what a lousy technique this is, just take a gander at David Mamet's wife, Rebecca Pidgeon, who is an incredibly lousy actor. I mean she's taken David Mamet's acting lessons for sure and every time you see her on screen you just go "Oh yeah, there's Rebecca Pidgeon, being Rebecca Pidgeon again." I mean, who cares? It's one thing if you're Katharine Hepburn, then you can be yourself if you want to. But if you're not Katharine Hepburn, then you'd better put on a fucking character and act.

So anyway, Nathaniel had read this and was all disturbed.

"I really agree with David Mamet that acting is all about just being yourself," he said, standing in front of me, "and then saying the lines. And that's what I'm trying to do. I want to be real onstage. I want to be honest. But I'm worried that if I'm just myself then that will be — well, gay. I mean I know I'm a bit effeminate. And I'm trying not to be homophobic in my acting. It's very difficult. I don't want to be fake — I want to draw on all my inner stuff, like Mamet says, but what if my inner self is, well . . . faggy? For want of a better word." Nathaniel did that shy self-deprecating thing he does, lowering his voice and casting his eyes aside. It was very appealing.

Well, I started off trying to tell him not to pay attention to stupid David Mamet, but I didn't get very far because he stopped me.

"No listen, let me try something. I want to just do something, I want to recite this poem and I'm just going to be myself, not do any sort of character, not do acting, and I want you to tell me if it's faggy."

"But —"

"No, please just let me try this, do you mind? I know I'm acting crazy, but I'm all crazy fucked up about this. Do you mind?"

"No," I said.

"Okay, here goes." At which point he stood opposite me, looking gorgeous in his loose-fitting pale blue shirt, his big dick swinging — I knew it was there somewhere in his pants — and proceeded to recite one of my favorite poems in the English language. "Let me not to the marriage of true minds admit impediments. Love is not love which alters when it alteration find . . . " Oh my God. I couldn't believe this beautiful young man was reciting it for me. He recited the whole sonnet. I watched him. Yes, of course he was being a little effeminate but that was one of the charming things about him. And that made it so beautiful. As I watched him,

I realized that a feeling was welling up inside of me — the feeling of wanting to kiss him. I didn't think about it consciously at the time, but that's what was happening. I realize now, I wish I'd been more conscious of what was happening and turned away.

When the poem was done he just stood there looking at me. I felt so sorry for him, trying to follow David Mamet's stupid acting directions and not be faggy. My eyes welled up with tears. I'm not sure whether he could see it though. I said, "Nathaniel, first of all, you just have to put David Mamet's stupid acting book in the garbage heap where it belongs. He's just a sad old straight guy trying to impress you and he doesn't know anything about acting. Acting has nothing to do with being yourself. If you want to read a good book about acting read Simon Callow's book, *Being An Actor*. He's gay and he talks about how acting is a mask, and how much he likes hiding when he acts. That's the exact opposite of what stupid David Mamet says, okay? You are you. You are Nathaniel and Nathaniel is a little bit faggy when he's himself because he's a fag, okay? If you have to do a straight role then you're going to have to act a little bit straight, okay? There's nothing wrong with that. And you can do that, I know you can, no problem, and no guilt for you in doing that. But you know what, I'd prefer it if you did gay roles like Hedwig because then you can relax and find stuff that you can't find when you're wasting time acting straight. But the main message I have for you is you can do anything you want, Nathaniel, because you're a very, very talented actor. So fuck David Mamet."

Then Nathaniel did something odd. Something that I completely misinterpreted. He took a few steps, threw his arms around me and hugged me. I could feel his lean hard body pressing against mine, and of course *that thing* in his pants. He hugged me very hard and then he pulled away slightly and said, "Thanks, Sky." But his arms were still around me.

And then I did it. It was the booze, it was Nathaniel's giant swinging dick, it was his blue eyes and his pale blue shirt. It was Nathaniel hugging me. What was I supposed to do? I kissed him. I pressed my lips against Nathaniel's and then I moved in to kiss him some more. It seemed to me to be something that was right and something he would want. He seemed to have so much affection for me, and he was so beautiful, and how could I deny myself this? How could I not go with the flow?

But boy was I wrong. Very wrong. Nathaniel pushed me away. "Sky, what are you doing?"

He had a horrible expression on his face. It wasn't just disapproval, anger, or hurt. It was disgust. Just plain old, blatant, visceral disgust. By doing this, I had caught nice Nathaniel in a naked emotional moment when he wasn't able to hide behind his usual politeness. His beautiful face was contorted with loathing and confusion.

"I'm just — I'm sorry."

"I don't understand, why would you do that?"

"I didn't mean to —"

And then he started shaking his head, gently. "No, Sky, no. That's wrong. That's wrong. No. Why would you think . . ." His voice became very calm, and smooth, but not in a nice way. "I've gotta go, Sky . . . I've gotta go . . ."

"Let me explain . . ." I said, which was a stupid thing to say because I don't know what the fuck I was going to explain.

"No, Sky, no . . ." he said as he went out the door and, after struggling with the lock, in a second he was gone.

It was like something out of Puccini's *Tosca*. I was Baron Scarpia. Scarpia the villain tries to rape Floria Tosca, but

72

instead she knifes him and gently places a cross on his dead chest. Scarpia is evil personified. He is so evil that when I saw *Tosca* in Toronto, there were child actors surrounding Scarpia onstage — and then the orchestra played the dreadful signature Scarpia chords for his first appearance, and all the children scattered, in horror. The children just sensed, they just *knew*, that he was evil. He had an evil aura.

Oh my God, what had I done? I had kissed the perfect, beautiful, innocent Nathaniel, who was the reincarnation of Larry Clemson. I had forced myself on a sweet young man whom I had mentored and who now thought he had to sleep with me in order to get ahead. And I had done it in our horrible tiny crack house fleabag Toronto apartment, standing in front of an ugly old mattress — he probably thought I had lured him there just for that reason. And the tea was still on the floor.

I was mortified, absolutely mortified. All the disgust that was in Nathaniel's face was now inside me. I was a goddamn monster.

The Next Thing

～

I didn't know what to do after the Nathaniel incident. I knew that I would never be able to work with him again. Every time I thought about it I was so horrified that I thought the only thing to do was not to think about it, which I know is avoiding the issue. I figured maybe all this was happening because my friends were deserting me and I was getting old, and there was no escaping the bitterness that comes with being a talented person whose work is neglected. All of that stuff was too big for me to fight so I just tried to put it out of my mind.

But I continued to do crazy things. And nothing I was doing actually had any serious consequences if I didn't worry about it, so I just tried not to.

My behaviour with my friend Miranda was not really so much bad as — well, it was just insane and came out of nowhere. And the whole incident made me lose her as a friend.

I've known Miranda for a couple of years. She was a friend of a friend in Hamilton and one day she just told me that she wanted to have dinner with me and talk about an idea to promote my work. Well, this sad old faggot is always open to any opportunity to get his work out there, so I agreed to have dinner with her.

I quickly realized that I didn't give a fuck about Miranda helping me with my work, but I really liked Miranda.

There was a bit of an odd connection there though.

I mean on the one hand our friendship made a lot of sense. Miranda was about 55 — close to me in age. Also, she used to work in the arts years ago, but now she ran a string of massage parlours (real, respectable ones). She had pretty well built the business with her bare hands. But she knew a lot of the arts people I did because she was a painter and film set decorator in the '80s, which is when I was doing all my theatre work. So we had lots of things in common.

The thing I loved about Miranda was that she could tell a good story. Boy, could she tell a story. And I really appreciate that. Not so much from men, for some reason, because I guess all men do is tell stories, at least straight men, that is. But what about when you hear a woman tell a story and she tells it as well as — or better than — some guy could? Not that there was anything masculine about Miranda. There was lots of power there — she liked to talk about "the mystical feminine," by which I think she meant sex appeal. She certainly had a lot of that. I wasn't actually sexually attracted to her, because I was never attracted to women, ever. But I could see, from a clinical perspective, that she was very attractive. Even though she'd had a mastectomy and had one breast removed. There are some women who just never lose that sex appeal. I mean they could have a hook for an arm and no legs but they would still be hot.

I could see why men went for her. She had shortish reddish hair and very bright pretty eyes, and a kind of round but not fat face with a pug nose. There was something twinkling and mischievous about her. She was half Irish and half First Nations, which is a pretty amazing combination of oppressed peoples.

Miranda was very sexual. A lot of her stories were about sex. This is where she reminded me a little bit of my mother, and this is also where the situation gets weird. You see I made friends with Miranda about six months after my mother died, and she seemed to me to be a kind of reincarnation of my mother.

I don't mean that literally. But certainly she filled a lot of spaces in my life that were vacated when my mother died.

As I said, I was abnormally close to my mother, and one of the things about her was that she was very sexual around me. I actually have always wondered whether there might have been some sort of incest going on between us when I was a child. I do remember sleeping in bed with her when I was a baby, which I know is odd. And then I remember her inviting me to come and watch her doing her exercises in her apartment in a leotard that showed off everything. I didn't want to be rude so I went — but I tried not to look. This was back in the '70s and my mother kind of looked like Mary Tyler Moore.

But the most incestuous thing about my relationship with my mother was that she told me way too much about her sex life. First, it was all about how bad the sex with my father was. She told me he was a premature ejaculator. Yeah, really. Does any kid need to hear that? From my father's point of view, my mother was frigid. I think that's just the way people talk about each other when they have bad sex. And remember, the bad sex produced me. I think people might be psychologically damaged in utero if they come into this world because of bad sex. But the point is that there's nothing more fucked up than a mother who tells you what a lousy lay your father is. And then after my parents were divorced my mother started a long romantic relationship with a married man. I was very conscious of these romantic evenings with her boyfriend because I'd be upstairs practising the cello when I was in high school and they would be drinking, smoking, and making out downstairs. (I only witnessed the making out by mistake once, but I knew it was going on.) And she just confided in me a lot about her sexual and romantic feelings, and why she was — and wasn't — attracted to certain men.

My mother was real femme fatale. By that I mean not only was she very beautiful (anyone can be beautiful), but she was always the most attractive woman in the room — and she knew it. She made sure that the men always wanted her, mostly by being aloof and brilliant in addition to being gorgeous, and not acting at all needy — even though she was, like, the neediest person in the world. So she was always a threat to other women's marriages, and she was damn proud of it. She divorced my father when she was 35, and after that, she became the dangerous divorcee, the 13th dinner guest, the hot chick you might regret inviting over for cocktails.

Well, in this way my mother and Miranda were very much alike. Miranda was the kind of woman who could walk into any party and all the women there would just put their hands on their husband's knee, or turn their heads away from Miranda and say, "Honey, it's time we were going." And Miranda knew it. She also had a habit of sleeping with married men.

Now I don't want to suggest in any way that Miranda was a home wrecker. She was certainly not. All the men she had sex with who were married either a) were already in the midst of leaving their wives, or b) would never leave their wives for her. What I'm saying is — and I think most people would agree — there's no such thing as a femme fatale at all, really. I mean sure there are sexy, horny women, but there's no way a woman can lure a man away from another woman unless he really wants to be lured — or unless the marriage is already a mess and the man is looking for it. One example would be that Miranda had sex with a married man for years just because he would never leave his wife for her, and she was fine with that, she was just in it for the sex. She used to call him her fuck buddy.

Miranda was actually really gay in a lot of ways. Dick size really impressed her. Because she was a woman, but, not only that, a *lady*, she always seemed to run into men with huge penises. It wasn't like she was looking for them — she just had an uncanny nose for news when it came to humongous phalluses. As far as I could tell her ability to discover gigantic members was unconscious, like a third eye or a keen sense of smell. (She was not alone in this. They said that Lana Turner's tits used to automatically point to the biggest-dicked man in the room.) Miranda said this about one of the men in her life: "Oh my God, Sky — it was just . . . it was just enormous. I couldn't let him fuck me because it hurt too much." I found that just too fabulous for words.

Well, one day we had quite the conversation.

We were both pulling back the cocktails, sitting on a patio somewhere on a sunny Hamilton afternoon, and Miranda goes, "I think we would have had very good sex."

"What are you saying?" I was kinda flabbergasted.

"I'm saying I think we would have been good in the sack, together, you know."

"Who?" I couldn't believe my ears.

"You and me."

"But that's not possible."

"Oh yeah, I know, like — you're kinda gay," she said, stating the obvious with a ironic smile.

"So why would we have sex?" I've always been very paranoid about straight women wanting to have sex with me. I had sex with women I didn't want to have sex with for like 30 years, before I came out.

"I'm just saying if we were to have sex, which I know we would never do, it would be like, stupendous, because we're both stupendous lovers and we would be great in bed together."

I wasn't going to argue with her. "Sure," I said.

Then she had to push it further. That was the thing with Miranda. She was very stubborn and she wouldn't give up, especially when she sensed that you had drawn a line in the sand. "We *should* have sex," she said, calmly, staring at me with an even gaze.

"What?"

"We should." She was expressionless, but I was waiting for her to break.

"You're kidding," I said.

"I kinda am." She took a sip of her drink. "And I'm kinda not."

"Are you serious?" I was really freaked out by the suggestion.

"Kinda," she said, and then finally broke. "I mean it would be a stupid idea because you know it might put our friendship in danger and I wouldn't do anything that would ruin our friendship so of course we wouldn't do it."

"I didn't think so."

"No, of course we wouldn't, dick brain." She paused. "And besides which, I wouldn't want you to think I was a fag hag." She looked at me. "Are you 100 percent sure that I'm not a fag hag?"

I couldn't believe she was asking this question again. She had asked me this question, like, 100 times. But that was something Miranda liked to do, ask questions over and over again, especially juicy contentious ones. It's as if she just liked to hear the answers again and again.

"I've told you a hundred fucking times that you're not a fucking fag hag. Do you want me to tell you why again?"

"Yes," she said, settling into her chair comfortably.

"You're not a fag hag because you don't fall in love with gay men. You don't need gay men sexually. Fag hags are sad lonely women who are often overweight and can't get sex because they think they're ugly. A fag hag hangs around with a fag not because she's friends with him but hoping that someday the fag will let his guard down and finally let her suck his dick. You're not like that, you have a healthy sex life with your fuck buddy, and you don't need to have sex with me."

"That's true." She paused and sipped her drink. "I still think we should have sex though," she said, stubbornly. And then the subject was dropped. Except that she still kept bringing it up practically every time we got together. Perhaps my mistake was suggesting that even if we had sex, she still wouldn't be a fag hag, and so that put the idea in her head that us having sex might be okay.

Boy, I wish I'd nipped that one in the bud.

But this was all part of the new me, the new "old" me, the me that was having trouble getting old. I was going through one of those periods at the time when the "Daddy" business wasn't too good. The blond that I always had sex with was getting really boring, and no one had pulled Daddy into a toilet lately and asked him if they could lick him all over. I was depressed about my sex life, and I was thinking, if only I could figure out a way to just get my rocks off with somebody on a regular basis, then I wouldn't have to spend hours cruising the baths.

Of course I could find a male fuck buddy, but that was always complicated. As soon as people found out I was Sky Gilbert (the semi-famous gay guy) it either turned them on too little or too much. They would be like, "I'm not having sex with Sky Gilbert." Or they would act like this one guy who, in the middle of sucking my cock once, stopped and said, "I just can't stop thinking about your plays." And I felt like saying: "Is my cock really that lousy?" I think it says something about my lack of sexual self-esteem that I didn't think, "Wow, that must mean my plays are fucking good."

Anyway, I was getting very discouraged until a crazy idea came in my head. Women had always been attracted to me and wanted to have sex with me. When I was straight I didn't want to have sex with women because I was forced into it — as I was closeted and it was the only option. Now it wasn't the only option but it was still, practically speaking — or maybe I should say *pragmatically* speaking — an option.

Why the fuck not?

It seemed that Miranda would be a good candidate. I mean she wanted to have sex with me and I knew that it wouldn't mean anything to her. I really didn't see any possibility at the time that it would hurt our friendship. I mean, she had fuck buddies, why couldn't I just be another fuck buddy? Sex didn't really mean anything to Miranda; she was like a man in that respect. I was getting kind of desperate and this seemed like a safe situation to give something new a try.

So one night we were out for a drink and I took her up on her offer. "So I've got this crazy idea. I think we should try having sex."

"Are you serious?" she said, peering at me over the top of her glass.

"Yeah I'm serious, why not. My sex life is pretty lousy now, maybe we could be fuck buddies now and then."

She kept her glass up against her mouth so I couldn't really see her expression. "I think it's a great idea," she said.

I explained to her that there would have to be a lot of boundaries. I wasn't going to want to do any kissing or hugging or foreplay. She was fine with that. I explained to her that my dick wasn't that big and she said it was no problem. (Women are nice that way. A guy might have said, "Sorry, I don't do under seven inches.") In fact I planned the whole thing out, laid out a plan and insisted that she go along with it. I told her that this was the way it should go. She would lay herself out on the bed. I figured we should do the missionary position because it was a basic starter position that hopefully we wouldn't fuck up. I told her she should probably wear a negligee or something kind of hiked up and lie flat on the bed. I would go into the bathroom and jerk off looking at my dick in the mirror to get myself hard. Then I would come into the bedroom with my hard-on and stick it in her, and fuck her until I came. I didn't want her doing anything much in terms of touching me and of course I wasn't into the kissing. I told her moaning would be good, very good. I like moaning. Of course I would be wearing a condom, and when I came I would pull out carefully and take the condom with me and go back to the bathroom and flush my stuff down the toilet. It would all be very businesslike. It could be subtitled "Sky

Gets Rid of His Load into Miranda," which is really all I was doing, and if she was fine with that I probably would be too.

She seemed fine with it.

We made a date for the next Friday night. I didn't buy her flowers or anything and I asked her not to make dinner. I didn't want it to seem like a date.

We started out in her living room. Miranda was dressed very tastefully, as I thought she would be. She was wearing a sort of lovely flowing Japanese housecoat sort of thing that covered most of her. I had brought quite a lot of vodka because I figured the drunker the better. I wasn't worried about getting a hard-on. After years of having sex with guys drunk at the baths I just figured, I could get hard enough to fuck somebody. And honestly I didn't think I could do this sober.

So we were quite drunk when I staggered upstairs.

I went into the bathroom and did my thing. At first it wasn't easy, but then I was so drunk that I started to really get into it. I started to think of Miranda as a cumbucket. I know it wasn't very polite of me, but after all I didn't have to tell her that — and it turned me on. I had seen lots of gay porn movies about male cumbuckets, who were guys that just lay there like the sex pigs they were and let guy after guy fuck them because they just liked to get the sperm in them. I thought of Miranda as one of these guys and it really started to turn me on. Just the practicality of it all. (Except of course I was wearing a condom so I was actually dumping my cum into that. Whatever.)

Well, I got semi-hard and I came out of the bathroom into the doorway of her bedroom. The lights were all dim. It was very Blanche DuBois. Miranda had covered the lights in the room with lovely pretty scarves and things so there were all sorts of different coloured but very dim lights on the walls. There were shawls and silky fabrics everywhere. She had brought me up to her room once to show me something on her computer and I had been very impressed about what a little fuck palace it appeared to be. Miranda was ready on the bed. She really knew how to do this shit. She was artfully placed in such a way that I couldn't really see her face (how did she know that would help?) and her kimono was pulled up so I could just see a bit of bush.

The only odd thing was that she was wearing nearly thigh high leather boots.

This was something I hadn't really counted on, but I tried not to let it freak me out. It made sense, in a way. Miranda was really into leather boots, she was always buying crazy red ones or black ones with laces — these ones were plain black. I mean I couldn't fault her for this. It wasn't necessarily a bad thing. It meant there was a little bit less flesh on flesh contact, which maybe was good thing as I was just into getting right into that cunt before my hard-on completely disappeared. And it made the whole thing kinkier, which was basically good. I figured it was Miranda having her own way in one small detail, because I had basically planned the whole thing out like a fascist and hadn't allowed her any input.

No words were spoken. I just climbed on the bed — which was very soft and comfy — and just put it into her and started thrusting.

Then the weirdest thing happened.

It wasn't that strange fucking a cunt. I remembered cunts and what they felt like. Basically, unlike an ass, they are just a lot better naturally lubricated, which makes you feel as if your dick is meant to be in there. That was the first sensation. I started to thrust and I could feel myself actually getting harder, which was, of course, a good thing. But then I realized a very bad thing, and it stirred an old memory about cunts.

They're kind of, well — roomy.

I mean I tried to increase the friction by pushing myself a bit forward on top of her but I didn't want Miranda to figure out that I was having a problem. So I just banged away. But the more I banged the more I realized that I was kind of banging into nothing. I thought of the Elizabethan term for cunt, which was "nothing" (accessing my old university research into Early Modern studies) and this seemed just really appropriate at this point. I mean it really struck me — how do guys get turned on by this? I mean there's all this space, you know? And does she even realize I'm in there? I looked down at Miranda and I couldn't really see her face as it was so dark. She wasn't making porn noises or anything, which was probably a good move because it would have turned me off.

The problem was the more I humped, the limper I got.

I should have just put this down to "failed experiment." But unfortunately I didn't. My brain always works too hard and I began thinking about Anastasia, my girlfriend for so many years, who I had fucked so many times. She was a big Ukrainian girl with child-bearing hips. I remember thinking at the time that she was really made for some big thick Ukrainian sausage, which I didn't have. I kept at it, but basically all I was getting off on was just the idea that I might get to come and treat Miranda like a cumbucket. But, leather boots or not, the whole thing just wasn't working. Maybe I had encountered yet another woman with a large cunt made for a bigger sausage. Miranda had some Russian blood in her too, so maybe that was it.

I finally pulled out and said it wasn't working.

I said I was sorry and I was going to go to the bathroom to clean up.

Miranda's voice stopped me at the door.

"Are you sure you don't want a blow job?" she said.

That was very nice of her to offer but I really didn't think it would help.

"No, sorry. I'm really sorry."

"You're sure?"

Jesus, why was she trying to talk me back into sex?

"No, I'm okay, sorry, it's my fault. I just —"

"Well, you were going pretty good there for a while. What happened? If you don't mind me asking."

"Nothing, nothing," I said, realizing how unfortunately appropriate that phrase was.

"It's no biggie," I said. But that was the problem, it was.

"Are you sure?" she said.

Jesus, what was it with the questions? I don't know why I answered. It was crazy, I was drunk, I've always had a problem with saying too much. I noticed when she was sitting up on the bed that she was wearing a wig, one of the ones she had bought when she came back from the hospital after chemotherapy. It was kind of charmingly askew.

Then I said too much. "It's just like it always was . . . I remember from my girlfriend, it's just, I guess I have a really small dick but it just seems that there's a lot of room up there . . . I'm not used to it." She stared at me blankly in her musical comedy wig. I continued. "I mean I probably just have a small dick. I mean . . . I know I do. I'm slightly below normal . . ." I thought I was being very polite at the time.

"Are you saying I have a big cunt?" She now looked pretty fierce and not funny at all.

"No, I'm just saying that I kind of forgot but cunts are generally big. Bigger than assholes. Nothing about yours in particular."

But she wasn't buying it. "You're telling me my cunt is big."

"No, I'm not, honestly."

"Get the fuck out."

I really thought I had covered all the bases by going on about what a small dick I had. I mean I could see some guy going on about how big a woman's cunt was in order to hide the fact that his dick was small, but here I was admitting that I had a small dick, taking it all on myself. But it didn't matter. There's no nice way to say words like that to a woman.

I left, shamefaced. Miranda was right.

Our friendship was never the same after that.

The Ultimate Degradation

~

I tried to look at my situation rationally. I mean, I had ruined a perfectly good friendship just to get my rocks off and all because I was paranoid about getting old. After all, one of my biggest problems was that I didn't have any friends, that my friends were deserting me because I wasn't nice enough and didn't listen. And here I had lost a perfectly good friend just because I had tried to use her to convince myself I was still a sexual being.

What lengths would I go to? If I looked at myself honestly, wasn't I just a very old guy doing everything he could to keep his failing sex life going — in fact, wrecking his life over it? Wasn't it time to throw in the towel and try to salvage the rest of my life?

It was then that I began to think about my boyfriend in the context of all these problems.

You might wonder why thinking about him didn't occur to me earlier.

Well, that's a big deal.

As I said before, my relationship with my boyfriend was not about being each other's "primary sexual fulfillment." The whole point was that we were a pair of sluts who got our sexual fulfillment elsewhere, and our love from each other. Under this plan, there was never any reason to demand more from him sexually or to involve him with my sex life. But I began to rethink this.

I really didn't want to rock the boat. My relationship with my boyfriend had always been incredibly solid, except for an incident that happened about seven years ago, when I kind of had a mini nervous breakdown.

It's very hard to explain. What happened was that I began to doubt our relationship.

Now it's another true thing about myself, one I didn't tell you, that I do have these maddening bouts of self-doubt that seem to come out of nowhere. I call it the Mary Tyler Moore Syndrome.

Though I am a super achiever like Mary Tyler Moore and somewhat famous (like her, in a smaller way), I have moments when I feel I'm a complete fraud and everything is going to fall apart. I definitely identify with Mary Tyler Moore in these moments, who used to think, "I'm America's sweetheart but I don't deserve it." For no reason of course. Of course she deserved it. She was Mary Tyler Moore. Well,

I go through the same thing she went through, and — like her — sometimes for no reason.

One late spring/early summer a few years ago, I went though a terrible period of self-doubt. It was at the 10-year mark of our relationship, so maybe that had something to do with it. Anyway, I was through with my teaching for the year and I had no plays to work on, and I couldn't think of anything to write. I got depressed and I thought I should turn to my lover to get me out of it. The other thing that happened was that my therapist was on vacation. That was actually pretty important. I was very dependent on my therapist, who was kind of a mother figure to me, and I think this may have had something to do with the crisis. (By the way, I don't see her anymore.)

Anyway, I went through this period where I wanted my boyfriend to solve all my problems and be my therapist. I wanted to be codependent with him. I understand now what was happening, but at the time I was completely lost and alone and it seemed that only he could help me. And I would get drunk and call him from the baths, crying, and say, "You have to help me. I'm in love with you. You must help me out with this." This didn't go over very well.

I know that may make him sound cruel, but looking back on it I really don't think that he was being cruel at all. I think I was acting like a child and asking him to be my therapist — but most of all I was really asking him to be my mother.

It was a test to see if my boyfriend would take the place of my mother.

As I said, I was always very close to my mother and I expected her to solve all my problems and she always did, and I always went to her and poured my heart out about my self-doubt and she would help me out. I wanted my boyfriend to do this too. When my boyfriend didn't act like my mother — and, well, mother me — I spun out of control.

I left him. I took the cats and put them in cat travelling boxes and got on the bus and moved into this horrible little room we were renting in Toronto. (This is before we got the crack house–style apartment we have now. Believe it or not this room in a rooming house was worse.) Looking back on it now, the whole thing was kind of comical. The big breakup. I called all my friends and said I was breaking up with my lover and it was all just so melodramatic.

I couldn't do it though because I loved him too much, and after talking with my therapist when she got back from vacation I realized that I was just trying to turn him into my mother, which was of course a big mistake. A boyfriend is not the same thing as a mother, especially a fucked-up mother like the one I had.

I'm telling you all this because what happened to me next was the ultimate degradation and it came close to challenging my relationship with my boyfriend. Because I lied to him. And I never lie to him.

I mean every time I thought of the idea of slowing down my sex life — or just giving myself a rest from all this promiscuity because I was getting old — I would think of the German doctor's plea in Larry Kramer's *The Normal Heart*. When she sees all the gay men dying of AIDS, she asks, "Why can't you just stop having sex?"

Jesus, I hate that play. Why don't *you* just stop having sex, you fucking Nazi? Do you know that Barbra Streisand bought the rights to the piece so she could play the German doctor? I'm sure she thought she would get the Oscar. People would say, "A Jewish princess playing a crippled German doctor. Barbra Streisand is no longer the 'Funny Girl.' She's brilliant." But no one would agree to direct Streisand in it and I guess she didn't want to direct it herself. So she finally sold *The Normal Heart* to HBO, and they filmed it with Julia Roberts.

I couldn't watch the damn TV show. A bunch of fags running around yelling — "I've got a purple spot on my foot, I've got the plague, I'm going to die." Jesus Christ. Get with the program. They just closed an AIDS hospital in British Columbia because there aren't enough patients. AIDS is basically over, it's a manageable disease, like diabetes. But for some reason people — and even fags — still enjoy watching movies where we are dying, and in agony all the time, and fearing for our lives. Don't even ask why. The whole thing is too depressing.

Anyway that "why can't you just stop having sex" line was written by Larry Kramer, an ugly faggot who couldn't get laid (that's why he wrote the nasty novel *Faggots* — sour grapes). And on top of that Larry Kramer was even crankier than I am now when he was young. So it was easy for him to say, "What's the big deal about sex?" Yeah, well, no big deal for you Larry, because you've got a face like a toothless homeless guy and nobody would want to live with you or get intimate with your egomaniacal self. But for those of us who actually *can* get laid now and then — well, we'd kinda like it if sex never went away.

That's the crazy thing. Here I am, 62 years old and there's nothing I can do to stop the tits from sagging (I can't have a publicity picture taken any more of my naked chest unless I cross my arms to pump up my tits), and my ass is dropping, and I'm getting those icky wrinkles (what am I going to do, get plastic surgery on my ass? *Please*). The only positive thing about having an old gay body is your balls get bigger. Or — at least — they hang lower. (Gravity.) But your nose gets bigger too. That explains why all the old men at the baths have hook noses and saggy sacks.

I know this picture is not pretty. But I can't stop. Fuck it. I *won't* stop. When I see that cute little thing bouncing along the street I still just go crazy. Not erection crazy — because I can't get them that easily anymore — just crazy. It's hard to explain. (Or not so hard.) Yesterday I was on the bus and I happened to sit down next to this guy and he almost gave me an erection, which is a big deal for me. I couldn't *believe* him. He was wearing a silver suit like a comic book hero. And he had a perfect haircut and a perfect Anglo-pretty face with a cute little nose and — oh my God — his suit was so tight it hugged his chest on the sides. And his hands were big and dark and tanned. At one point his thigh touched mine and I was in some sort of heaven. I mean this guy was a god, a Greek god, and I would have done anything for him. But, of course, most of all what I wanted to do was have him sit on my face. That's what I call real intimacy, having a cute young guy rub his ass in your face. There's no way you can get closer to anyone, trust me.

I'm not ready to say goodbye to all that.

Which leads me to the ultimate degradation.

It started innocently enough, when I saw the "closed for renovations" sign on the coffee shop where I usually hang out on Church Street. So I had to go to another one. This was a big deal. You see coffee shops are where gay men hang out these days. It's the '60s all over again (but without the drugs and the sex — though you can get those too, you'll see what I mean soon enough). So gay men are doing their dating mainly online these days — even though they still go to bars, baths, toilets, and parks, just not half as much as they used to. Most gay men cruise for men on gay sex sites like Grindr.

But you know it can be lonely cruising Grindr on your cell phone at home. And what if your phone says "There's a hot guy only 20 feet away from you" and then you have to get all dressed and then go find him? Much better to do your internet cruising at a café where the guy who says he is 20 feet away from you is actually sitting across the café. And guys do cruise without using cell phones in coffee shops. Sometimes it's just about sitting and modelling — and looking like you're picking people up on your cell phone — or having chats that turn into sex later. Trust me, stuff *is* going on in these places. So I used to go to the Starbucks upstairs on Church Street because that's where all the cute boys hung out. Well, when they closed the Starbucks to renovate it, that meant that I had to hang out at one of the "old guy" coffee shops.

Me and other old guys. Well — they look at me with suspicion, most of them, because they can tell I'm not one of them. By that I don't mean that I look younger than them but that they can sense I'm not a usual old guy *type*. First of all, I've always identified more as a girl or a boy than a man. The idea of being an old guy is that you're totally embracing being a man. Because now you're double the experience, double the sagacity, double the gravitas. But I've never even thought of myself as a man: I identify as a girl or a boy but not a man, so when I get with a real "man" type guy, which is what a lot of these old seniors are — or imagine themselves to be — I'm fucked. You see because I come off as vulnerable and girlish or boyish, I get sucked into listening to their crazy boring old-guy stories. I know, it's nuts. I've lost all my friends because I talk too much and don't listen, but if some old codger comes up to me, I'll listen and feel too embarrassed to excuse myself. I don't know what it is — I'm just scared of hurting their feelings I guess.

Also I'm scared of them coming on to me. But I'm not totally age-phobic. I have sex with older guys (i.e., over 40) now and then at the baths, but they have to be super hot dominant tops who really know how to abuse me and order me around. I'm not into heavy s/m but I do like someone who tells me what to do, and treats me like shit, and puts me on display, and appreciates my body. I love all that stuff. And occasionally you'll meet some old Daddy master-type with extended nipples. (How do these old guys get such big nipples? They are amazingly extended — very sexy . . .) The kind of guy who knows exactly how to touch you and talk dirty, and cup your balls in his hand when he's giving you a hand job, and that's heaven. That really is heaven. But the boring ugly old guys — it's a nightmare when they come on to you.

I tried to be friendly with older guys. I tried to make friends with this older man who hangs out on Church Street all the time. He's just like me in some ways. (I try to remind myself that I probably look as old as he does, because hey, I forget.) I mean I suppose he's not bad looking — bearded of course, not fat or anything, always dressed casually. He fits in — sort of. And I always see him talking to young guys (unlike myself, he's not shy). Well, here we are, two old guys hanging around the same scene night after night and not talking. I mean, are we competing or something? So I chatted him up for a while. But then he started griping about being forgotten, and about all he had given to the community, and how bitter he was, and how under-appreciated he was for all the great shit he'd done in his life, and — Jesus. I just thought — no, I can't do this. I hate bitter old fags. I mean, I'm a sad old faggot, which is different. I'm not bitter. I accept my abjectness. Well, maybe I don't accept it, but I *acknowledge* it, anyway.

And I don't expect the young to fucking *respect* me. I know I'm old and look pretty useless, and everything I did was just way before your time, and you don't give a shit.

So you don't have to admire me, okay? Just fuck me. Is that asking too much?

Despite all these misgivings about old guys, I finally decided I was going to be hanging out at the old guys' coffee shop — because basically I had no choice. So I sit down and do my typing and I'm actually feeling pretty at home, and no old guys are telling me their crazy boring/bitter stories or coming on to me. I'm fine. Then this guy sits down next to me. Wow. I can't believe it. I mean he is just the type of stunning guy that turns my crank. And he's *old* according to my standards, maybe like 40 at least. And he has a little silver in his hair and a very kind of rectangular face with a very straight up haircut, and just . . . I don't know how to describe him. Very masculine features, beautiful brown eyes, *perfect* stubble, and a body that's not all built up but is definitely *there*. And he's sitting beside me and I'm getting horny from the proximity. I can't help slyly glancing over at his computer, now and then. And on the screen are photos of people. Some men, some women, some young men, all fully clothed. And he's doing some sort of Photoshop thing. It strikes me that he's a photographer or some sort of visual artist. But I guess being a photographer is a lot more like being a visual artist these days because they can fool so much with the colours and everything on computers. Anyway, I glance over now and then and hope that he notices that I'm glancing over and sure enough, he finally says, "Excuse me."

He's got this great way of talking. It's very high school football coach — which of course is a great move for him, very masculine, but friendly, keeping his cool, calm and collected, but smiley and nice. All this is turning me on even more. And he says, "Sorry to interrupt you, I notice that you have a Mac and I was just wondering if you know how to turn a document into a PDF." Now though I am basically computer illiterate, this is one of the few things I actually do know how to do.

"You just go to print," I say.

"Oh — you go to print?"

"Yeah, you go to print, and it asks if you want to save it as a PDF file, and then you can just save it as a PDF file. It's pretty simple."

"Oh wow." He tries it out on his computer as I watch him. "That's great, thanks." He kind of salutes me. And that military-ness — again — works like a charm.

We both went back to our work and that was all we said to each other that day. But each time we were both at the coffee shop, we acknowledged each other with a nod. Then one day we ended up sitting beside each other again. And I thought: "This guy is so hot, and he started a conversation with me about a stupid PDF, why the fuck can't I initiate a conversation now with him? It's my turn in the flirting cycle, right?" So I said something inane like, "Excuse me, I happened to notice on your computer that you are dealing with a lot of photos there. Are you a photographer?"

He seemed pleased to chat. "Well I am, sort of . . ." he said. He made it clear that he was an amateur photographer as well as a part-time actor (that bit irked me). I asked him what he did acting-wise and he said not much, but that he had been a stand-in for one of the actors on *Rabbit Hole*, Greg Bryk. We chatted some more and he revealed that he had a son (within the first couple of seconds, actually) and told me a little about his photography and how tough it was to get anywhere. He said his name was Pete. Then I decided to take fate into my own hands. I thought this guy was nice enough to maybe be a friend so why not pursue him — not just out of lust, but as a person? And besides, I needed some photos of myself. I always need photos of myself for the back of books and stuff.

So I asked him if he'd be willing to take some photos of me. I told him I couldn't pay him much but that he'd get the photo credit. He seemed very interested and enthused. He told me that he liked to take pictures at Allan Gardens and that he would phone me. We exchanged phone numbers.

When I got home I looked up the actor who he was a stand-in for on *Rabbit Hole*. Greg Byrk was definitely very hot and they definitely looked a lot alike.

Well, he was on it like a fly on shit. In a couple of days I got a text from him — "Can we meet sometime this weekend at Allan Gardens? The weather is supposed to be nice. I have to see my son in the afternoon so maybe in the morning?" There was that son again.

Was he fucking straight? Hanging out in a gay coffee shop?

We agreed to meet at 11 a.m. on the Saturday morning in a coffee shop near Allan Gardens. He was a little bit late but texted me — very responsibly — and I began to realize that he was a very responsible fellow. Very — seemingly anyway — courteous, present, responsive, nice, honest. It sure seemed that way. It wasn't a very hot day but it was May and he was wearing very fetching shorts and a T-shirt. He was the type of guy who looked good in anything.

Soon after he sat down I asked him if he was gay. I thought it was a reasonable question.

He was straightforward, but he wasn't straight. "I'm bi — basically, I'm just open to things," he said, which was a good enough answer to justify me lusting after him. We talked a little more personally, or at least he did. I was afraid to reveal too much about myself because I didn't want him to know that I was well-known because he was an actor, and he might have heard of me. He said at one point, "I took the liberty of googling you to see how you'd been photographed in the past."

Well, the cat was out of the bag.

It was interesting the way he talked about himself. I mean, it probably should have been one of the warning signals. I think it's important to be very careful when people either give signs of, or admit to, being a part of a 12-step program. Now he never said that he was in a 12-step program, but he just seemed a little bit too fucking sensible and healthy. I was talking about the fact that I was shy about being photographed because I'm very vain and I always think I look ugly, and about how I'd been a fat child with a bad self-image. Then he went on about the opposite situation, about being young and being taken advantage of by a lot of attractive older men because he was so fucking beautiful. (He didn't say it was because he was beautiful but it was pretty evident that this was what he was referring to.)

Now I'm usually attracted to stunners, and used to dealing with all their neuroses about being stunners. But then he said, "I went through a bad period," which is kinda like a warning signal. I'm not saying that people should avoid socializing with people who go through "bad periods" (after all I just told you about *my* bad period). It's just — well, it's probably just good to flag the fact that the person you're dealing with might have serious addiction issues — because if you don't, then later it might come as a big surprise, okay? Then he talked about getting balance in his life, and eating all the right foods, and really wanting people to respond to him as a whole person, and living in the now. I really should have known at this point that there was a 12-step thing going on.

Anyway after breakfast (I paid, because he was going to take photos of me) we went on to Allan Gardens. Well, it was there that the ante went right up. I don't know how many photo sessions you've ever been involved in, but they can easily get weird. First of all with some photographers — once they get me alone — they seem to get very intense, and start clicking away madly and asking me to do what I consider to be somewhat weird things like taking off my clothes a bit. It's very important in these situations to keep control and not let the photographer go nuts or you'll end up with crazy naked pictures of yourself on the web. I think photographers act like this because of my semi-celebrity status. These guys (usually they're guys) are thinking, like, "I've got Sky Gilbert and I'm getting him to do crazy things. Then I'll take pictures of other semi-celebs doing crazy things, and I'll do an exhibit first online, then in a gallery, called 'Celebs Do Crazy Things,' and it will be a huge success." I just know that's going through their heads and I'm onto it, so I usually take control and don't let them get me naked or do any other crazy stuff.

The problem with this guy was that he didn't get all intense and hysterical like that. He was totally in control in a really sexy way that was turning me on unbearably. It's like the whole photo session was a big sex scene and he was the top and I was the bottom. I mean, when he took the photos it was like we were having sex.

So as soon as he gets there he starts putting me in front of flowers — which I thought was a great idea. I told him it was great to have a contrast between my severe face and the flowers. And he says, "So that's how you see yourself, as severe?" And I say yes, and that people are always expecting me to be a dominant top and that I am a real pussycat inside. "Ah, give me that dominant top look," he says. So I give him a few and he clicks away. "Yeah, I get it," he says. "I think it's appropriate that I'm on my knees," he says. "Makes me want to get down and do 10." I didn't really know what to say but the mention of 10 made me think of, you know — inches. Then he flicks a piece of fluff off my face. "You don't mind if I touch you?" he says. "No, not at all," I say, trying desperately to communicate that I want very very much to be touched by him all over my body. I'm wearing a leather jacket with pockets in the chest area. He begins to play with the little silver tab on the zippers that are on each pocket. "I think we should move them over," he says. And he starts to move them. The silver tabs are just above my nipples and it really feels as if he's trying to make like he's playing with my nipples — not just the tabs on my coat. And he knows it, because he looks me straight in the eye as he fiddles. I'm getting a chub-on. Then he says, "Listen, I want to try something, and I hope you don't mind me saying this, but well, I'll just say it . . ." He gives me his winning smile again: "I want you to look at me as if we just had sex. Let's say we just had sex. I want you to give me the look that would be on your face after that. Just show me everything. Show me it all."

"Okay," I say.

He moves away and starts clicking. I don't know what the hell an "after sex" face would be, I just give him all sorts of satisfied smiles, hoping he will get the message that sex with him would be ultra-fabulous in my estimation. And of course during that part of the shoot I am so turned on that I am practically coming in my pants. I can't imagine what the photos looked like. They must have been ridiculous.

We went to several other areas with flowers and he took shots of me with different lighting and stuff. When it was over he said he had to go meet his son and we were sort of awkwardly standing out front of the conservatory. And I was feeling like we'd just had sex, and like I wanted to set up another date. And then I thought, why not risk it, if he rejects you it's his fucking fault because he is such a fucking flirt, he's totally asking for it. So we were talking about financial arrangements around the pics, and I told him I'd pay him $50 when they were done and then I just blurted it out. "You know, I'd really like to play with you some time."

Oh Jesus. I said it.

I thought "play" sounded much more relaxed than "fuck," and I figured he would get the idea.

His feet kind of shifted back and forth. "Well, I'm pretty much really sexually screwed up right now ... kind of in a strange place." I wasn't sure what that meant. But of course I still wanted to fuck him no matter how screwed up he was. In fact I wanted to even a little bit more. "No problem," I said, not to sound pushy. "If not we should get together anyway, see a movie or something." That was a good move. In fact it was the clincher.

"Sure, why not, let's play." He looked at me levelly again. I was so sure he would dominate me and it would be so fucking hot. "The only thing is ... I don't have a place, though." Oh, fuck. Now normally in this situation I would just suggest we get a room at the baths. Because of course my lover and I have an agreement that we don't use our little pied à terre in Toronto to fuck people. But I knew that a bathhouse tryst wouldn't go over too well with this Bisexual-I've-Got-To-Meet-My-Son-In-An-Hour-Type-Guy. So I did a crazy horrible thing. I said: "I've got a place."

"Oh great," he said. We set up a date to meet out front of my apartment building in Toronto the next Friday evening.

Then we shook hands.

My hand was shaking after because I couldn't believe what I had done. I had made a sex date with someone at our little crack house apartment. This was something I had told my boyfriend I would never do. But I was coming to a point of no return. I wasn't angry at my boyfriend — or trying to get back at him — or at least I didn't think I was. I just thought "Here I am, getting older by the minute, and this hot guy wants to have sex with me and the only way it's going to happen is if I use our fucking apartment so why the fuck can't I do that? Fuck you, non-codependent boyfriend." Those were my feelings exactly.

And besides, I didn't see any reason why my boyfriend would ever have to fucking know.

I almost cancelled the whole thing several times. But then the next Friday I found myself at Winners buying linens. That's how crazy it was. I was actually going to fix up the apartment. And this was a double lie because I had promised my boyfriend that I would fix it up someday so that it would just be a nicer place *for us* to stay — but now here I was doing it because I knew my new bisexual fuck buddy wouldn't want to have sex in an apartment that looked like a crack house.

The apartment actually looked almost nice when I got through. I even bought a throw rug to match the only comfy chair and a lamp. And since there were no curtains, I hung a funky tie-dyed sheet across the windows. I figured I could tell him that we had ordered curtains especially custom made and we were waiting for them to come (that sounds like a very gay thing to do).

I'm very resourceful.

I felt guilty and horrible all the time I was doing it. But I was sex obsessed, walking around with a chub-on for the whole day thinking about him. Surely my boyfriend would understand. (Not that I was planning on telling him.) I mean the only reason we didn't have sex with people at the apartment was because we didn't want the sketchy people we have sex with to know where we lived. What if one of my fucked-up tricks ended up knocking on the door one night when my boyfriend was there. How pretty would that be?

But this guy wasn't sketchy. Or I told myself he wasn't, ignoring all the signals about his 12-step background.

I bought lots of vodka and mix and was already a bit drunk before he came. I dressed up in the only outfit I trust myself in — my lucky black tank top with the cut out arms to show my tattoos. It hides my belly and looks kind of alternative. I also wore my trusty ripped up pants.

It was the same magic outfit that I had worn the night the crazy Daddy-lover had kidnapped me in the toilet at Woody's.

Pete was wearing a casual shorts and tank top outfit. I noticed that he had a nice leathery type backpack slung over his shoulder. I never noticed it at the coffee shop. This was a trick bag if I ever saw one — in other words, he'd brought along kinky equipment. What the fuck was in that bag?

He smiled sweetly and seemed full of the same centred, grounded energy. I led him up in the elevator and when it was going up he looked around approvingly and said, "Ah . . . mirrors . . ." I thought I was going to come in my pants again. Honestly, if he had told me that I had to get naked and come out into the elevator with him and have sex in front of the mirrors I swear I would have done it, I was so turned on by just standing next to him.

When we got to the apartment he looked around and said, "Nice place." And I said it wasn't really. "We're ordering curtains custom made," I said, doing the nod to being a normal fag.

"Cozy," he said. "Do you mind if I make myself comfortable?" I told him sure and that I was going to make myself a vodka and tonic. Did he want one? No, he didn't drink. Another bad sign. Those who don't drink often . . . get very high on other things. I went into the kitchen and poured myself a double. I could hear him taking things out of the bag. Jesus, what did he have in there? Did he do poppers? I had vowed never to do them again, several times, but I could certainly change my mind again for him.

When I came back he was sitting on the bed on the fancy gold coverlet I had bought especially for him. He had laid a couple of things out on the bed for me to see. There were some poppers, sure enough, and some lube, and condoms, and something that — well, I wasn't sure what it was but I had a feeling. It sure looked like one of those electrical devices.

I haven't really mentioned but I've always had a fantasy of participating in what they call electro play.

In case you haven't heard of it, there's a wand that you can buy that shoots out tiny little electric currents. Nothing that could hurt you, but it titillates in just the right way. Usually the wand is put against the nipples, or the dick, or the balls and you get a tiny little shock. It's kind of like being tortured, but it's not. Whenever I saw a video with such a thing in it I would go crazy.

I even subscribed to an electro-play website once.

When I saw the "wand" I couldn't believe it. It was like he had read my mind and knew not only that I was a bottom from hell, but exactly what kind of bottom I was. I sat down in the chair next to the bed. "What's that?" I asked.

"What exactly?" he said.

"You know that . . . that wand thing." I was gulping down my drink very quickly.

"You called it a wand, I think you know what it is."

"Well I do, kinda."

"It's for electro play."

"Oh yeah," I said, gulping. "I've heard of that."

"You have?" he asked.

"Yes," I said.

"Take off your clothes."

Jesus, how did he also know I was an exhibitionist? I wasn't even worried about getting a hard-on, which I usually am at the baths. I knew I would be hard enough as I was so fucking excited. I undressed very quickly and stood there, ass to the air, dick rising. "Nice nipples," he said. "Nice tit ring." He paused. "Would you like Daddy to nibble on that ring?" Oh my God. He was going to be Daddy. That was so great. It was such a relief not to have to be the fucking Daddy.

"Yes, Daddy," I said, my dick filling up with the humiliation of calling him that.

"Stand opposite me." He proceeded to bite very gently on my nipple. My chest felt fucking huge. I had put on a cockring before the whole evening started, and my dick was raging in it. "Oh My God," I said. "Oh God . . ."

"You like that?" he said.

"Yes, I do, Daddy . . ." I said because I knew he would want to hear that word.

"Looks to me like you might be ready for another sensation. Are you ready for the magic wand?"

It didn't even seem corny that he called it that.

"Yes, sir — ah, Daddy," I said.

He smiled in that tough but sweet sergeant way he had. I noticed that his smile was a little crooked. It was very charming. "No, call me sir," he said softly. "I'd prefer it if you called me sir."

It was all the same to me. "Yes, sir." I said. He lifted the wand. He turned it on. Little sparks came out if it. I shivered.

"Like that?" he said.

"Yes, sir," I said.

"Are you ready?" he asked.

"Yes, I think so, sir." The wand moved towards me. "What exactly are you going to do, sir?"

"Oh you'll find out," he said. He guided the wand over to my nipple and held it there.

A little jittery current came out and my nipple jolted from the burn.

"Ah," I said. Oh Jesus, I was never so fucking excited before in my life. I was jerking off now and getting rock hard. He stood opposite me, looking very handsome and continuing to apply the wand gently to my nipples. And then he moved it down to my balls and I thought for a minute I was going to come. But then I thought before I came I had to have it from him, I had to have my ultimate intimacy. I wanted him to sit on my face. I knew he would have a big hairy man's ass, and I knew I could take it, and I knew it was all I would want and then I would come.

And so I asked him. "Sir," I said, "would you . . . would it be all right if you sat on my face?"

"Is that what you'd like, boy?" he said.

"Yes," I said, nodding. "Sir, that's what I would like."

"Sure, boy. Anything you like. I just want to ask you a little favour. If I'm going go sit on your face then maybe Daddy would like to do a little treat himself."

"A little treat?" I said.

"Yeah, just a little —" He put down the wand and pulled a pipe out of his bag. "Just a little of Daddy's medicine."

"Daddy has medicine?" I said, stupidly.

"Yes, and Daddy just wants to do a little medicine. If his boy doesn't mind."

"No," I said, shaking my head, even though inside I was thinking, "Oh no, so he is a lapsed 12-stepper." "No, I don't mind," I said.

He took off his shirt, and his pants, and he appeared to have a hard-on in his underwear, and he was wearing it straight up. His body was just as I expected. It was full and hard, some hair on his chest, not built up, but manly and fucking sexy. Big hairy legs. Big hairy ass. Just what I wanted to get my nose into.

He pulled some little crystals wrapped in plastic out of his bag and put them into the pipe. Then he pulled out a light and lit the pipe, sitting in the chair. I was still standing up.

"Feel better, sir?"

"Oh yeah, Daddy likes his medicine." He stood up and yelped once or twice. "Yeah, yeah, Daddy really likes that." This was a pretty strange deviation from before. He suddenly had all this drug energy. But then he calmed down and became the cool daddy again. I wondered if it was crack or meth. I'm not really an expert on drugs.

He picked up the lighter and the pipe and said, "Follow me."

Of course I did.

He was leading me towards the bathroom.

When we got there he told me to get into the bathtub and lie back, which I did.

Then he got up on the edges of the bathtub, putting his feet on either side of the edge. This looked really risky and even though I was very turned on, I had enough sense to ask him.

"Do you really think that's safe?"

"Yeah, boy, yeah, that's safe as safe can be." And then he lit his pipe and took a couple of puffs, his ass staring me in the face. He started to lower his ass onto my face. As he lowered it he dropped his metal pipe and the lighter into the bathtub. He was spreading his cheeks. The bathtub was pretty well lit but I couldn't see what was in there. It looked pretty dark and hairy.

Finally he got down on my face and I couldn't believe it. This guy was so — this guy was so fucking clean cut and handsome and his fucking ass was filled with shit. I'm not kidding. Some of it was crusty and some of it was just, well, shit. I started to choke, and I tried to push him off my face and he just kept grinding down, but I was freaking out and I pushed him off his perch on the tub, and he was very stoned I guess and even though he landed on his feet, thank God, he also went straight into the opposite wall and hit his head on the wall and then kind of slid down the wall to the floor.

Jesus Christ, I thought he was dead.

I called an ambulance.

I had to clean the shit off my face.

Making Some Changes
But I'm Not Sure What

~

What followed was really an awful period.

Pete didn't die or anything. At least when the ambulance took him away he was kind of nodding and rambling, and after that I didn't hear anything from him. And I figured somebody would have told me if he was dead.

There was no reason why my boyfriend had to know anything about what happened. I hid all Pete's drug stuff when the ambulance people came — and the wand and his trick bag — and Pete never contacted me after the hospital. I didn't have to go to the hospital because I got Pete out into the hall (that was fun) and told the ambulance guys that I had found him out there. Stoned guys did used to sneak into the apartment building and walk the halls, a lot of them crack types. So I just told them Pete was one of those guys.

I didn't feel guilt about pawning him off like that. I mean the guy said that he had gone through a "tough period" in the past, so obviously he was in total denial about being a crack addict now. So maybe this would be a turnaround moment for him. Was he a total liar? I'm not sure. The only thing that made me think maybe he was telling the truth about being bisexual and having a kid was the fact that his asshole was so dirty. No self-respecting faggot would have had such a dirty hole.

But I wasn't guilty about him. Or even what I did with him. No, it was that I had kept the whole thing from my boyfriend. And again, there wasn't any reason to tell him about all my little problems. It wasn't like we were codependent or anything. But this was something that could have affected our relationship. I was breaking our rules. And this was a sign, as far as I was concerned, of a serious mental breakdown. I didn't know what I was going to do next, after forcing myself on some poor innocent big-dicked actor who came to me for help, and trying to have sex with my female best friend, for Christ's sake, and then using our sacred apartment for a drug tryst. And I felt like I couldn't tell my boyfriend about it, or I shouldn't tell him because he would break up with me if I did.

Again, it was like I wanted my boyfriend to be my mother. And even though I'd been through this before with him, that didn't make it any less urgent. I felt like a helpless little kid who'd done a bad thing. I just wanted Mommy to make it right. But I knew going to him with all this shit would also be just dumping crap on him, and asking his forgiveness would just make him mad.

The same day I was dealing with all this shit, I got a phone message from my father. He told me that he had mailed me a whole bunch of crap from my past — memorabilia from him and my mother.

It seemed like a crazy coincidence.

My mother had died a couple of years earlier, and I guess my dad still had some stuff he had collected from her. My dad was 88 years old at the time, and he lived in a seniors apartment in Buffalo. I guess he was just cleaning up.

When I got back to Hamilton from my crazy Toronto night, a parcel was waiting. I didn't know if it was a good time for me to dive into this all this old stuff, but I just did.

It's always weird looking at pictures of your parents when they were young. And my mother married my father when she was 17 years old. He was 21.

But what interested me much more than the pictures of them were the pictures of my uncle. My father was an insurance salesman and his brother started out being an insurance salesman — in fact they both worked for my grandfather's agency — but my uncle got bored with the insurance business and studied to be an engineer. This was one of the reasons why I always thought my uncle would make a better father than my actual one. Nothing against him. I love my father. I mean everybody loves their father, right? But my father was a businessman — he moved on from working for my grandfather (nobody could work for my grandfather) to being a salesman, and then a manager for Travelers Insurance. I'm a fucking leftie, not a capitalist; my father's life was devoted to making money. But my father's older brother had a calling, a trade — he was passionate about something besides making money.

In some ways, my uncle would have made an ideal father for me. He was a handsome, natural-born entertainer. He and my aunt even took part in amateur theatricals. In the pile of stuff my father sent me, I found this photo of my uncle, his wife, and my mother all dressed up for some sort of amateur play in Connecticut, where I was born. My uncle's wife (I think she was his future wife at the time) was dressed up as an old lady in a wheelchair. My mother was just playing a pretty girl I guess. And my uncle was dressed up as a cop, which looked very sexy on him. He was holding the wheelchair that held his future wife. And he was looking straight out at the camera. And my mother was looking up at him. My father was nowhere to be seen.

I know this was just a play. But the way they were posed seemed to me to suggest the way things might have gone in real life. You see, my uncle's wife was a very butch, fat, unattractive woman who everyone thought was a dyke (in fact both of her sisters looked just like her and were in the military). No one could ever understand why my uncle married her. I mean sure, she had a lot of personality (you could tell by the picture of her as an old lady in a wheelchair), but she wasn't very attractive whereas my uncle looked like Paul Newman. It seemed to me he would have been a perfect match for my beautiful, charismatic fucked-up mother — not his own wife.

Now that crazy photo set in my mind the crazy idea that my uncle was really my father.

Maybe it was because I had just seen that movie by Sarah Polley, you know, where she finds out that her real father is not the charming, underachieving actor she has known her whole life, but instead, a writer, filmmaker, political radical, and a Jew. Sarah Polley was real lucky. I mean, wouldn't you want your father to be a controversial lefty intellectual who tried to change the world more than a kind of sweet actor who didn't change anything?

Maybe in the back of my head I was thinking that her

movie wasn't wishful thinking, it was the truth, and the same sort of thing could happen to me.

You might ask why I would go on this tangent all of a sudden, trying to get a new father.

Well, in case you haven't noticed, I am having a hard fucking time getting old. And part of the problem for me is that I spent 30 years in the fucking closet, trying to deny my attraction to men. So now here I am, 62 years old, and it seems like I have to start denying myself sex like I once did again, just because I'm old. Does it make any sense to you that part of my identity is all wrapped up in being a slut? And that I don't want to give that up? Because that means giving up who I've been for 30-odd years? The new self I discovered when I came out? Am I just supposed to throw all that away? Can I even do it?

The other thing about us gays is that our parents can never be gay. You get it? Nobody ever thinks about this. (I don't know why.) It's kind of like the famous barber's paradox ("In a village, the barber shaves everyone who does not shave himself, but no one else. Who shaves the barber?") No truly gay person can conceive a child — if they do then they are bisexual at least. So every gay person has straight parents. This just doesn't seem fair to me. Now my parents were so straight that they didn't get along. By that I mean they were typical of straight culture, you know "men are from Mars, women are from Venus." But what if my father hadn't been my father but my *uncle*? And what if my uncle was a *gay man*? Or at least a playboy and a kind of actorish person? After all, my uncle's wife looked like a dyke and *he* looked a lot like Paul Newman. Maybe they had a marriage of convenience. All they had was daughters, his wife never gave birth to a man-child — doesn't that sound like the family of a dyke and a gay man? I know the evidence is kinda weak and it's sort of stupid-assed thinking, but . . .

I think I thought there was something about this whole thing that would help me to stay closer to who I am. Or justify my crazy behaviour. Or something.

Or it could just have been that I was getting old and, like all old people, I was getting interested in my "roots."

So if I went to see my uncle, and tried to figure out (by asking subtle questions) if he really was my father, then I would also be able to talk about getting old with my faggot father.

Then there were those letters.

When I found the letters I thought, "Could this be the reason why my father sent all this stuff to me? Could this be the whole secret reason? To unload information that was unsettling to him?"

Packed at the bottom of the photographs, and held together with a rubber band, were some odd letters. There wasn't much writing in them — that is, in terms of words. They were more like cartoons. Each of them was addressed to my mother, "Dear Patsy" (a nickname my mother used at the time). The cartoons were crazy. They all told little stories. The stories were about a young man courting a young woman. The young man was very handsome, and a lot was made of this in the cartoon. His hair was slicked back and he was always wearing a suit. He was a caricature of someone tall and dark and handsome (very much like my uncle). And the girl looked a lot like my mother did at the time. The cartoons told the story of the young man always getting into absurd scrapes, situations that interrupted his attempts to make out with the girl. Like when he picks a bunch of new flowers for her. But by the time he gets to her door, all the flowers have wilted in a charming way. The cartoons were actually pretty witty.

And in the cartoons, Patsy would always forgive her handsome hero no matter what. These seemed to me to be *for sure* cartoons that my uncle could have made up. I mean my father never showed an ounce of artistic talent, but my uncle was an amateur actor and a fabulous storyteller. And the stories he told were always about his "men" — the men who worked "under" him. I remember visiting my uncle and he would always start reminiscing about the old days as an engineer, and how he got his "men" to follow him. (Almost as sexy as Christ and the disciples.) And it sounded like the guys he used to work with were still, to this day, fucking crazy in love with him in a mentor/acolyte way. It was almost like they were an army outfit that had done battle. My uncle, whose name was Charlie, used to hold meetings of "The Charlie Club" once every year or so with all the guys who used to work with him and their wives. Well, by now all the members of the Charlie Club except for one had died, and yet this one old guy (who lived in Las Vegas) would drive across the country once a year to have a drink with my uncle and reminisce with him.

Sounds pretty gay, eh?

Maybe I'm grasping at straws. But these cartoons were obviously written by some guy who was not my father. The only catch in my theory was that the cartoons were signed *"H."*

But maybe it was some sort of code, right?

I also figured that if I went on a trip, I would break the pattern of self-destruction I seemed to be in (somebody with a shitty asshole falling on top of you in your bathtub can do that). And if I stayed around home, I would end up telling my boyfriend what had happened in the Toronto apartment and that would fuck up *everything*.

It wasn't that hard to make the trip. There's a train that goes straight to New York City from Hamilton. I always spend a couple of dirty nights in Chelsea (I love Chelsea) and then take a train to Norwich, where my uncle was staying in a seniors home.

The only thing was I would probably have to see my uncle's two daughters, who always drove me crazy because they were perfect.

I knew it was a long time traveling so I had to find something suitable to read on the train. I'm a real fan of the New York Review Books, and sometimes when I can't find a book to read, I just look through the list of books they publish and pick one. So this time I'm looking through it and I notice that they've just put a new book on the list: *The Other* by Thomas Tryon. And then another crazy coincidental thing happens. I remember that my uncle once told me that he knew Thomas Tryon.

Thomas Tryon is a pretty fascinating character. He always interested me because my uncle said that he knew him. Like my uncle, Tryon grew up just outside of Hartford, Connecticut (about a half hour from where I was born). His father used to run a men's clothing store called Stackpole Moore Tryon (it's still there). Well, for a while Tom Tryon was a big movie star. He used Thomas as his writing name, and Tom as his Hollywood name. He was actually quite a big leading man in the '50s. His two biggest roles were as the lead in Otto Preminger's *The Cardinal* and as the gunslinger Texas John Slaughter. But he was also in a lot of famous B movies like *I Married a Monster from Outer Space*. Well, after making about 10 movies in the '50s, Tryon suddenly quit and became a writer. Just like that he switched over and went by Thomas instead of Tom. And his first novel — *The Other* — was a huge fucking hit.

I remember seeing pictures of a very handsome Tom or Thomas Tryon and thinking, "Wow, didn't my uncle say he almost worked with him at my grandfather's insurance business in Hartford?"

So it just seemed important that I buy the fucking book.

I ordered it from Amazon and it came in a day.

It made me look forward to the trip because I really love the train; I love just sitting all day and reading and writing and listening to romantic music.

Well, I wish I could say that I liked *The Other*. I didn't.

The experience of reading *The Other* on the train was very disturbing and exciting; and I wish I could say it was because it was so good.

Okay, spoiler alert. I'm going to tell you about the big plot twist in *The Other*. But does it really matter? I mean they've already made a movie of it and the book has been around for ages and, frankly, it's a dumb book. The plot is this: there are two brothers, a good one and a bad one (the "other"), and the good brother doesn't know what the fuck to do because his bad brother keeps getting into trouble and basically, well, killing people. So as you are reading it, you are thinking, "Should he tell his parents that his brother is a killer?" (I've never had a brother so maybe brothers don't betray their brothers or something.) But this aspect of the novel reminds me of one of those horror movies where the hero and heroine are going down into the pitch-black basement and you want to yell, "Don't do it, you dumb fucks." But if they didn't do it, there would be no movie, so nobody yells that. Anyway, for some reason the good brother doesn't tell anybody about the bad brother, but then you find out the *real reason*. Are you ready? (Hold on to your hats!) The good brother *is* the bad brother. I'm sorry I spoiled it for you, but I honestly thought it was a pretty corny plot twist point and frankly I could see it coming from a mile away. So you spend the whole first part of the novel wondering why this kid doesn't turn his bad brother in. And then when you find out that the one brother is really the evil brother in denial, you're supposed to be in this unrelenting state of horror about watching all his evil deeds, because you had identified with the character in the first part of the book. Get it? Ugh.

Sorry, but that's not what happened to me.

Instead I was horrified by how fucking sentimental the novel was. It was filled with heartwarming scenes — the good little boy is always hanging out with his grandmother and bonding with her in cornfields, and making brownies and Russian stews. And the grandmother has magical powers and . . . I just can't go on. I mean New York Review Books is trying to tell me this is a well written, dark, existentialist modern novel, but it's actually just a feel-good thriller with a trumped-up plot twist.

But because the novel was so bad, I was pretty detached while reading, and since I had "Is my uncle really my father and is he gay?" on my mind, I couldn't help noticing that this novel by his fucking friend Thomas Tryon was actually pretty gay. I mean, you read *The Other* and you are getting a fucking gay read. You could even wank off to it. I almost did.

There is an especially gay scene where the two brothers (before you know that there is only one brother) are lying on a dock — on a perfect summer's day of course — and they're both blond, and nude, and have lovely tanned skin and lithe young bodies that are kissed by the sun, and it's just all very homoerotic. First of all, you start thinking, "They should be fucking." And then if you go back and read the scene when you know that there are not two brothers but only one, then you think the brother wants to fuck himself (which, in its own way, is also very gay). Now you put all this together with a boy who truly loves his grandmother and who has a very dark side that he is afraid of, and basically you have a gay life story. What I'm saying is *The Other* is basically a gay novel for straights, and maybe that's why it's such a horror story to most people, and why I don't find it horrifying at all.

After I figured out the novel was gay, I got obsessed with figuring out if Thomas Tryon was gay. Sitting on the train riding past Syracuse and — as always on that trip — thinking how lovely the old Syracuse station was, I was glad I had my computer. And thank God they had Wi-Fi on the train so I could google Thomas Tryon. His Wikipedia page is suspiciously short. I say *suspiciously* because it seems to me that something important might be left out. I looked for what most people take to be a sign of heterosexuality — i.e., whether or not Thomas Tryon was married. Well yeah, he had been married but only for two years. What's that about? Who gets married — and it was late in life, when he was like in his mid-30s — and only stays married for two years? And they had no children. And then he died, unmarried, in 1993. Of stomach cancer. But cancer could be AIDS, right? But the most incriminating thing about him was the picture of him when he was old. He was just too fucking attractive to be straight. He did not look like an older straight man. He looked like a fucking gay man with a super clean a-hole.

So let's say Thomas Tryon was gay, and he was my uncle's friend. As far as I was concerned, the plot was thickening.

When I got off the train in New York I was in a state of excitement. I went to the Museum of Television & Radio to watch old reruns of *Texas John Slaughter*. Tom Tryon was not only very handsome but definitely gayish in his manner-isms. The reason I say this was that he was actually not a very good actor. He looked like he was struggling with the same thing Nathaniel was struggling with when he came to me for advice. How can I be "real" as an actor when my real self is a nelly queen? I mean Tom Tryon was definitely holding back, and he seemed sensitive in the same way Montgomery Clift and James Dean were sensitive, the only difference being that he wasn't as good an actor.

That night in New York City I wiped out all my tension and stress by sitting myself down drunk on the floor of one of the cubicles of a little sex club in Chelsea (it's a video store with rooms at the back) waiting for some guy with a big cock and poppers to shove it all in my face. I got so stoned I'm not sure if sex really happened, but it sure seemed like it did, which I guess is the same thing.

The next morning I was very eager to get on the train to Connecticut and very glad I didn't decide to stay more than one night in New York City, because now I really wanted to see my uncle more than anything. The trick was not to insult him, or anger him, or kill him by mistake with my questions (he *was* 92), but to find out for sure finally whether he was a faggot or not and even, maybe, my father. I thought that even if he didn't tell me, once I sat down in the same room with him and looked him in the eye, I would know.

I made arrangements for my cousins to pick me up in New London, the closest spot to my hometown of Norwich.

Of course they were very glad to see me. I don't know what to say about my cousins except that they completely intimidate me because they are perfect in ways that I am not. They are years apart, but they still seem like twins. And when they were young they were like the good twin and the bad twin in *The Other*. My cousin Terry was a tomboy and always mucking about in the mud. Her much older sister Sherry (there are about 10 years between them) was a straight-A student. Well, now Sherry is a Greek teacher and Terry is a born-again veterinarian.

I guess I'm exaggerating about their lives being perfect. But they are wholesome and all-American and skinny, blond, pretty, and perky in ways I could never be. Sherry and I are both university professors, but of course Greek is a much more respectable thing to teach than theatre. Whenever Sherry talks she's bragging about winning an award or how much the students love her. Actually she doesn't even brag, she's modest, which is almost worse.

My students don't love me, which I know is my own fault. I guess they might find me entertaining, and they might learn something — but I honestly don't think they love me. I'm not that *special* teacher who changes your life. It's not that I don't try. The problem is that I'm a big old faggot and very sexual and I am very scared of being chummy with the kids because if I did I might end up telling all my private shit and the kids might think I was coming on to them. There, I said it. Now I would never fucking come on to one of my students, but there's all sorts of stuff in my books and on the web about my sex life and what a slut I am, so I have to be careful. I mean I've had male students who have suddenly started chatting me up after class about something that I did in drag in some cabaret. And I know they're looking at me wondering, "Are you okay with everyone knowing this stuff about you? Should I tell the rest of the class, the ones who for some reason haven't googled you, that you're a slutty drag queen in your spare time?" Some of the super cool male students are jokey with me about being gay but in a too-familiar way that seems to be crossing a line. It's not that I hide the fact that I'm a drag queen slut, it's just that I don't talk about it when I'm teaching. To make a long story short, I try to be a good teacher but there has got to be a pretty big boundary between me and my students (especially the male ones) because I'm the only out slutty drag queen faggot teacher they're probably ever going to have and that puts me in a vulnerable position.

Of course Sherry doesn't have any of these problems. She's an adorable heterosexual woman who probably hardly ever has sex and is the best fucking Greek teacher ever and the students all love her, and want to be her, and she takes her students on trips (which I could never do). And they're always giving her teaching awards. And now her son wants to be a perfect Greek teacher like his mother.

And Terry — well, she just drives me fucking crazy. I mean she and I used to do boy things together. (She was more of a fucking tomboy than me; she took after her dyke-ish mother.) I just remember going off into the woods with her and digging in the mud, playing with frogs, and building forts, and whatever. So what happens when she grows up? She becomes a veterinarian, a super soccer mom for her two boys, and religious. Oh God I hate that. I mean she doesn't push it (they never do, do they?) in the sense of "You should go to church more often," but she sure mentions church a lot. I mean every other comment is, "Our church group is doing this," or "The kids are going to Japan with the church group." Terry actually went to China at one point to help teach religion to Chinese people. I'm serious. Don't they have enough problems in China without having to deal with Christ? So on top of it all, Terry's a kind of missionary, and I can tell that she's looking at me and asking me about my "partner" and what he does for a living, but deep down she thinks I'm an Asshole-Licking-Child-of-Satan.

And even if I am some of those things she thinks I am, it doesn't mean I don't resent her thinking them.

My dad's always loved it that Terry's a veterinarian. It's a profession he really respects and can relate to. Is this because there's just something so lovable about animals? Who knows, but all of her veterinary stories keep the family in stitches. And when I try to tell them my stories, the punch line always involves a tranny friend of mine, or teaching sexuality to students, or something that makes the whole clan go silent as they all ponder the fact that things like sex and trannies exist in the world outside Connecticut.

To top it off, on this visit all my cousins could talk about was the Grand Canyon in Arizona. After spending five minutes with them I thought that if I heard one more word about the Grand Canyon I was going to puke up my Amtrak Nathan's hotdog and Entenmann's cookies. It turns out that for my uncle's 93rd birthday, my perfect cousins were taking him to the Grand Canyon to celebrate. This is something I had never ever thought of doing with *my* father. And I feel so fucking guilty about it. And my father had been saying over and over, "The cousins are taking Uncle Charlie to the Grand Canyon," obviously completely unable to hide his jealousy. I know he desperately wanted *me* to take *him* to the Grand Canyon, but there's no way I'm going to do that. I mean, what the fuck would I say to my father if we went there?

The thing that drives me craziest of all about my father is that we have absolutely nothing to say to each other. He always asks me about school or about all my theatrical "successes," which, as a topic, doesn't last long. And then at some point when the conversation flags, he always says: "I just wanted to tell you that I really think your mother did a wonderful job of raising you." I always agree with that, because

I don't know what else to say. Then he adds: "I just want you to know how thankful I am that you are not a murderer or a drug addict." I never know why he picks these two particular things to focus on. I guess it's because I'm already a homosexual — and those are the only two bad things left for me *not* to be.

Just imagine the scintillating banter we'd have if we went to the Grand Canyon, after he'd exhausted congratulating me for not being a criminal.

"Wow, there's the Grand Canyon."

"Yup, Dad, there it is."

All I feel is guilt, because Charlie's children are such perfect daughters. And I'm a lousy, disappointing, childless son, who doesn't fear God and doesn't teach Greek.

I tried to make it all go away by reminiscing with my cousins about the good times in the car on the way to Norwich. New London has all these memories for me because it's where we used to go for summer vacation when we were kids. We lived in Buffalo before my parents were divorced, but we always went back to Norwich for the summers. It was something like a Thomas Tryon novel back then. What I will never forget is going down to Osprey, which is just south of New London.

Osprey was a private beach club. And my parents and my uncle's family — and even my grandparents — were members. They used to go there when my dad and uncle were kids.

Each day in the summer we would arrive at about 11 in the morning and spend the first hour or so setting up. We rented beach umbrellas and big red tables with tiny feet that we stuck in the sand. The sand was pure white. And then we would play in the water, usually torturing snails, poking at dead jellyfish with sticks, and snorkeling in shallow waters. In no time it would be lunch and the parents would haul out the sandwiches and potato chips that they'd brought for us and we would sit at the red tables and eat lunch. The trick was not to get sand in your sandwich. Then you had the arbitrary hour-long wait before you could go back into the water again.

This was my favourite time. We would take a leisurely walk to the lighthouse at the end of the beach. It was on a lonely rock. But first we made a stop to get an ice cream bar from the Good Humor man, who always rang his bell at 1 p.m. After our ice cream bars, we would walk really slowly because it was all about digesting lunch. And we would kick the sand, and chat about everything and nothing, and just gaze out at the sea. Then we would walk back to the parents and ask them if it was all right for us to go swimming yet.

After the walk came the big project — swimming out to the wooden floating raft, about 50 feet from the beach. Beside it was a floating miniature lighthouse. Swimming to the raft was very exciting because we had to swim through eelgrass — long green tendrils that would get tangled in our legs if we didn't keep completely horizontal. I was very freaked out by the eelgrass, and when we were swimming through it I would yell, *"Eelgrass, eelgrass."*

It was deliciously scary.

I didn't tell anybody, but my big fear at the time was not so much the eelgrass but the idea of swimming on top of a huge open space. As I got into deeper water I would imagine the crazy depths under me and all the ugly creatures living down in the dark that were swimming past my legs. But basically it was just all that space. Like the Grand Canyon.

At the end of the day we were so tired in just the right way, and so we would wander over under the wharf that housed the wooden lockers where we kept all our stuff. Or

I would sit in a deck chair on the covered wharf and watch the sun getting lower. We were just kids. But we knew that at night the teenagers would come with their barbecues, setting up evening parties in the dark. It was something that we couldn't participate in because we were too young. But we could wonder.

I'll never forget those summers. And as I drove through New London with my cousins, we played the game we used to play as we got nearer the beach as kids. Whenever we saw the ocean we yelled out, "I see water" in anticipation of all the fun we were going to have. And it came out "Icy water."

As we got closer to my uncle's seniors building I began to worry about getting him alone and what approach I was going to use to find out if he was gay without killing him.

My perfect cousins had been nice enough to rent me a room in the apartment building — they had these, like, hotel rooms for relatives of the seniors to stay in. It was a very classy place. So I just figured that after my cousins left I would have some time to talk to my uncle before he went to bed and that I could figure out a way to ask him stuff without upsetting him too much.

My uncle met us at the front door, which I thought was pretty amazing. He had oxygen on a little cart, because he has trouble breathing. But amazingly, even for 92, he still looked — well, maybe not hot, but Paul Newman–ish. He was very tanned and always had giant sinewy hands and very kind eyes that were a warm shade of blue. The best thing, of course, was that he was still a joker, always telling stories, turning everything into an anecdote. He had some very entertaining things to say about his aquafit classes, about finding a frog in the pool, and about how he'd smuggled in a gift for the aquafit teacher, who was an attractive young guy. (I knew he was attractive because later in the apartment Uncle Charlie showed us a photo of himself with the teacher at the pool.) The girls brought grinders with them. So we sat down in his pretty little living room with the big picture window that looked out on a quaint Connecticut forest scene and devoured our lunch.

You may not know about grinders. They are another fabulous reason to come to Connecticut. I'm not sure how they make them. Once I actually looked up the ingredients and tried to make some for myself. They are just subs — but they are the best fucking subs you have ever had. I think the secret is slivered lettuce, provolone, prosciutto, and just the right amount of olive oil in the dressing. But whatever it is, it's like love — it's something you can only find in Connecticut and nobody can really tell you how to make it.

Then we talked and talked about the grandchildren and how proud my uncle was of them. And I did a lot of oohing and aahing about everyone's achievements and tried to talk about mine. But most of my achievements are in the past and as they have to do with the performing arts, they were kind of hard for my uncle and his perfect daughters to understand. But being in the same room with my uncle, I felt drawn to him in the same way I had as a child — drawn to his kindness and gentleness (he was not at all like a normal "guy" in that way). I noticed that he would carefully address certain questions to me, and ask me a lot about my partner, which I thought was pretty open-minded (or *something*!) for a 92-year-old of his generation.

As the evening stretched on I figured out the cousins didn't want to leave me alone with him. I mean, it was going on nine o'clock and this was the point that I could see an old guy like him tiring, and the cousins were making no move to leave without me, just going on some more about the Grand

Canyon. And I could just see the two of them getting up at some point and saying, "Well, I think Dad needs some rest, so shall we show you down to your room?" So I decided to take the bull by the horns and just blurted it out: "Hey there's some stuff I wanted to talk to Uncle Charlie about, is that okay?"

But they forced me to say the word "alone."

"You mean . . . alone?" said Terry.

When I said yes, Sherry looked worried. I could tell Terry was ready to be the Christian nurse and say, "I don't think he's up to it," so I jumped in with, "It's really no biggie. I just wanted to talk to him about Dad and you know . . . I'm interested in stuff about when they were kids, you know . . . No big thing." Which was all basically a lie — but I'm not a theatre guy for nothing. Sherry gave a kind of careful approving nod, and Terry finally gave her pursed-lip approval.

So they trundled out after lots of cautionary recommendations about this and that, and Uncle Charlie's oxygen, and confirming the date for his next appointment with the doctor, and finally, finally they were fucking gone.

My uncle was very kind and innocent, not suspicious at all, and I noticed that when it came down to it, he did look very old and vulnerable. Maybe I was seeing the young man in a mask over the old man, because now that I had him alone his eyes seemed very wide and sort of detached from his face, the way the eyes of some very old and/or dying people are. But I wouldn't be put off.

"So what did you want to talk about?" he asked — after he finally got himself into his chair and his oxygen arranged beside him. There was interest in his voice and just a little bit of concern. I told him I was just really interested in his early days before he became an engineer, when he and my dad used to work for my father in Hartford.

"Oh yes, that was back in the late '40s, you know when we got back from the war and your grandpa wanted us to work for him. But as you know, it didn't work out."

My grandfather wasn't a very nice man, and he alienated all of his children in one way or another. But all I wanted to do was ask Uncle Charlie about whether or not he knew my mother back then. Charlie launched into an anecdote. He sure was a storyteller.

"Did I ever tell you about Katharine Hepburn?"

"No," I said.

He sat pretty stiffly in his wingback chair, but I could tell he was enjoying himself.

"Well, I tried to sell her an insurance policy, by accident. It went like this. I was doing door-to-door at the time. You know, going to people's houses and speaking to them directly. And so I knocked on the door of this one house, and a lovely young woman answered the door, and I told her that I was selling insurance policies, and she invited me in. She really was beautiful, but it didn't register in my mind who she was. I mean, what shocked me looking back on it was that she was so polite. She listened to my whole little pitch, you know, and she was very nice about it, nodding and asking questions, just like any normal client. She let me go to the end of my sell, and I was pretty new at it, so I don't know how good I was, but I got all the way to the end and then she said, 'I'm very sorry, but my father has already taken care of this.' And so I thanked her for listening and then I left. And it was only when I was walking home that it occurred to me you know, that I had been talking to Katharine Hepburn."

"Wow," I said, because I didn't really know what else to say. This was supposed to be an investigation and the anecdote didn't quite fit into my investigation plan. On the one hand I supposed that it might have been a very gay thing for an old man to be obsessed with the memory of a female movie star. But of course the way he talked about her was the way any old straight guy would. I decided to change my tack. "So we passed by Osprey today," I said.

"Oh yes, it's still there," he said.

"You know I really love that place," I said. "I'd love to hear more about what it was like when you were young. You know before you were an engineer, when you were both selling insurance, did you and Dad used to go to Osprey, with your girlfriends and stuff like that?"

"Oh yes, it was a really social place back then. And we would go down at dinnertime you know, and set up a barbecue, and bring girls there."

"What girls did you see there?"

"Well, I used to take Peg there, before we were married, and your father at the time was dating Phyllis Wilson, and Camilla was there, and her brother, and you know some of our friends."

"Was my mother there?"

"Pat? Not so much. Though I did see her there a couple of times. She was pretty young, you know, only 16 I think, when we first met her."

"Did you ever date my mother?"

"Me? No, I was pretty much dating Peg — she called herself Margaret at that time. We were pretty much together from the moment we met."

I felt that I was grasping at straws. The fact that he met his dykey wife and latched on to her at an early time could have meant that he was a real closet case, but it could also have meant that they were just madly in love. I tried once more. "So you didn't know my mother very well?"

"No, I didn't. I'm afraid I hardly talked to her at all. She was a lot younger than me, you know — close to your dad's age. She was kind of an outsider to the group. Because she didn't really come from our social scene. Her mom — your grandmother — was a divorcee, you know — some people didn't approve. But Patsy did used to hang out a lot with Tom, though."

"Who?"

"With Tom. With Tom Tryon. He used to join us sometimes."

Wow. I controlled my excitement at the mention of Tom Tryon's name.

"I think you told me that you used to know him once."

"Well, I didn't know him really well, not way back then. But I got to know him later when he applied for a job selling insurance with my dad."

"What was he like?"

"Well, Tom seemed like a really nice guy. He and his brother Lane. They used to hang out with Camilla and Patsy, because Camilla and Patsy were very beautiful girls. I mean Camilla used to be this platinum blond, she looked like a model. Your mother must have shown you pictures of her because she was your mother's best friend. And the Tryon boys, well, they were just as good-looking in their own way. They were really good-looking guys."

I really tried to read something into this but the way he said it was so matter of fact that it didn't work.

"Were they?"

"Oh yeah. They looked like models. In fact, they used to work at their father's store, at, you know, Stackpole Moore Tryon, and they would sell suits, and they would wear the suits when they were working in the store because they looked so great in them."

"So let me get this straight." I tried to control my excitement. "So my mum and Camilla used to go on double dates with Tom Tryon and his brother?"

"Well yes, I guess you could say that — it was as close as a double date could get to that. When we were young back then, you know, when we were dating, we would hang out in groups."

I knew that I had come there to ask him about his relationship with Tom Tryon and to find out if my uncle was gay and if maybe he was my father. But an idea suddenly hit me. My mother used to go on double dates with Tom Tryon. Maybe it wasn't my uncle who was my father. Maybe it was Tom Tryon.

I was so excited by the idea that I got anxious. You know when you think of something that might be true, and you hope it's true, and you hope so much that you get very excited and scared that it might not be? This happened. I thought I was going to faint. I got up and started to pace the room. My uncle said: "Sky, are you okay?"

"Oh sure," I said. "I'm just . . . tell me," I said, sitting down again, trying to look calm. "Do you think my mother and Tom Tryon could have been romantically involved?"

"Well, I never thought of that," said my uncle. "I mean, I guess they could have been. She didn't start hanging out with your dad until about a year after that. I knew Tom after he almost got the job selling insurance with us, but when he didn't, your granddad hired your father instead. Your grandfather always wanted to work with his two sons, you know. And after Tom disappeared, that was when your dad met your mother. And you know it happened pretty quickly, between your father and your mother. They were married six months after they met. On your mother's 18th birthday. And then they had you, just nine months later almost to the day.

You know I even joked with your dad 'that was a close one buddy,' because you know if you had been born any earlier, then there would have been talk."

I found myself speaking out loud, not able to control it. "But I was a month late."

"Oh, you were?"

I don't think he was too eager to think about the idea that I might have been conceived out of wedlock.

"Yes," I said. I got up and started pacing the room again. "Let me ask you something else."

"Sure," said my uncle. I realized that his very even way of talking was, of course, related to his age and his difficulty speaking and breathing, and it was not easy to discern what emotions he was going through, if any.

"So you said that Tom Tryon applied for a job working at my grandfather's insurance agency?"

"Yeah, he did, as I said, we offered him a job, yes, but he wouldn't take it."

"Why?"

"Well, we were very disappointed because he would have been a great guy to have on our team. He was so, you know, presentable. People liked him, men and women. People were drawn to him. But you know, he was kind of too good-looking to be an insurance salesman. He really had that star quality, even back then. But when he found out he'd have to stay in Hartford, he didn't want the job."

"No?"

"No, he was very clear about that, he said that he didn't want to stay in Hartford, he wanted to work in Springfield. You see, your grandfather had just opened a branch of his insurance agency in Springfield."

"So he really wanted to transfer out of the state?"

"Yes."

I was pacing now.

"And when was this that he left Hartford? Was it around the time that my father and mother were married?"

"Well . . ." He thought back. "Yes, as a matter of fact it was. Right when they were getting married. I think it was actually the day before or . . . no maybe a couple days after."

"Oh Jesus," I said. It was a eureka moment.

My uncle expressed concern, not so much in his expressionless voice, but in words. He said again: "Sky, are you sure you're all right?"

Of course I was all right. I was more all right than I had ever been before. And now all of a sudden I felt as if I was going to be reborn. It was that serious.

I thanked my uncle for his kind help and lied. I told him I was writing a novel and working on an idea and that I was getting emotional because I had just gotten an idea for it. Saying things like this to people always works because they are so confused by the idea of creating a novel and have such romantic ideas about writers and writers' lives that they will pretty well believe anything. And they don't want to go *there*, don't want to get into inquiring about your "creative process." Most people are pretty mystified by the whole thing, and I think probably scared by it, and it shuts them up.

I reminded him that I had to get up early in the morning and get the train back to Hamilton. I knew he was pretty tired and probably relieved to get rid of me. As I went back to my room, I almost got lost. This seniors building was like a maze, and each wing had a different name like "Trafalgar" or "Littlefield" or "Fox Corner." It was a very white place, where white people die. Each of the names referred to a different wing or "community." But if you didn't know the building, it was really easy to get lost. In the back of my head was what my own father had told me about the place, and the reason he didn't ever want to live there. Apparently the apartments — "Sunset Estates" was the name of the complex — had all these lovely suites to live in, yeah, but they were just kind of a cover. If you were to look at the building from the top, you would see that all of the wings surrounded a central area. You couldn't go into that central area unless you were authorized. What was inside there? You guessed it. A hospital. Twenty-four-hour care with beds and medical staff. So if you suddenly dropped semi-dead they would sweep you up and take to the hospital. The whole "seniors apartment building" thing was kind of a front for a hospital, which was where, if you were lucky, you might end up (meaning if you got there you weren't, at least, dead). My father knew about this and so did Uncle Charlie, but my dad was like, "I'm not going to that seniors building, it's the same as going to live in a hospital," which was true in a way, but that was the whole point — that people wouldn't have to worry about their elderly parents suddenly conking out. In my father's brain it meant there were orderlies waiting just behind all those hidden doors — like vultures — for you to drop down sick, so they could scoop you up and get you on a stretcher.

Anyway, as I wandered the halls in my confused and excited state, I couldn't find my way from "Harvard" to "Dover." I kept taking the right turn that said "Dover" — which was supposed to lead me to my little hotel room — but it would for some reason always take me back to "Harvard" again. I really wanted to get back to my room and google some stuff about Tom Tryon. As I kept traipsing the same hallway over and over I would pass doors with signs that said

Do Not Enter in really bold letters. I knew what that meant. I knew they were the doors to the secret hospital lodged at the centre of this place (it was kinda shaped like the Pentagon but with a juicy deadly centre). I thought, "Why don't I just bang on one of those doors?" Because then one of the orderlies would open it up, all eager for a medical emergency and hoping it was time to gear up and take another sad unlucky senior to his final bed of pain. And I would say, "Which way to Dover?" which I pretty much figured would be straight through to the other side — if I could just get there by walking through the mysterious middle.

But I didn't do that. Finally after a pile of frustration I figured that once you got down one of the hallways that said "Dover, Willowtree, and Beach Place," there was a little sign that said "Dover" that you had to take or else you would end up going all the way back to "Harvard" again. When I got back into my hotel room I settled down on the bed and went back to the Wikipedia for Tom Tryon. Because now the truth seemed obvious. It wasn't my uncle who was my father.

Tom Tryon was my father.

All the evidence pointed to it. He used to double date with my mother, and then suddenly he's not anymore, and he wants to get out of Connecticut, and my mother suddenly marries my father, and the baby was probably conceived before my parents were married. So *you* figure it out.

I was so excited. I needed more proof. I googled Otto Preminger, the director of *The Cardinal*, the last movie that Tom Tryon ever made.

There was a long description of all of Tryon's trials and tribulations with *The Cardinal* on an IMDB link. Preminger was famous for being dictatorial and a lot of people hated him. He had to be king of the set. (His biography is called *Otto Preminger: The Man Who Would Be King*.) His big thing was humiliating actors.

There's nothing more horrible than a director who humiliates actors. You have to understand this. It's not like you're working at a job at Sobeys and you get yelled at by the produce manager. Not that working at Sobeys would be a dream, and sure, I'd much rather be an actor than stock produce at Sobeys (even though I'm not very into acting and don't do it much) — but when you are humiliated by a bad boss in a normal job, you are not putting your emotions on the line. I mean if you are stocking the produce at Sobey's, and your boss comes up to you and says, "You idiot, you forgot to clean the carrots," you can just go all really silent and give him a false smile, because carrots are not a part of your emotional life. A play or a movie is different. If you aren't laying your emotions on the line, then you're not a good actor. Some gay directors humiliate male actors. Especially directors who are old and ugly — they like to humiliate the cute boys who would never fuck them. Now Otto Preminger wasn't gay, and he didn't humiliate Tom Tryon because he was trying to fuck him. But there sure was some weird thing going on, some demented father/son torture/masochism thing. Tom Tryon wanted to be in that movie, and it was a big prestigious part, but if Otto was treating him that badly, there was really no reason he couldn't have fucking quit the film if he'd wanted to. But he didn't. And more than that, when it comes down to it, all he had to do was stand up to Otto Preminger to stop the abuse. Other actors who worked with Preminger said all you had to do was stand up to him and he would back down. In fact, Otto actually liked it when actors challenged him. So what stopped Tom from putting a stop to the abuse?

On the first day of shooting of *The Cardinal*, Otto Preminger fired Tom Tryon. But not only that, the first day of shooting was in Hartford, basically Tryon's hometown. Tryon was so proud of himself for having gotten a leading part in a big serious Hollywood movie, he'd invited family and friends to the shoot. And Preminger fired him for no reason in front of his whole family. So Tryon, completely humiliated, went down to the basement of the church they were using as the dressing room to change before leaving. Preminger followed him. "What are you doing?" he asked. And Tom Tryon said, "You just fired me. I'm going." And Preminger said, "You took that seriously? Jesus, I was just kidding."

You get the picture. Tom — just like me — had the Mary Tyler Moore Syndrome. Here he was a big gorgeous movie star, but all it took was an abusive ape like Otto Preminger to make him feel like a piece of shit. And you know why he didn't stop the abuse by standing up to Preminger? Because deep down he knew he was a piece of shit and deserved it.

He was *fucked*.

So much so that it was very clear to me that I *must have* got this fucked-up gene from Tom Tryon. The gene says, "Beat me, humiliate me, tell me I'm an asshole because I can't believe I'm worth anything." If Tom Tryon was my dad, it all came together, it all made sense. I think the reason why I was so into the idea that Tom Tryon was my biological father was because then I would know what it was like to have a father who was flawed like me: a father who could admit to being a scared, lonely, and fucked-up effeminate mess. Because if I had a father like that I would hug him and I would say — hey, I'm like that too.

But as I thought this, I also thought I was completely crazy to think it.

But I couldn't stop. Was I becoming Blanche DuBois? She knows what it means to be a liar, what it means to *lie to yourself*. By the end of *A Streetcar Named Desire* Blanche is lying about everything, about her hope, about dreams, about life. Everything is made up. And they cart her off to the nuthouse.

Was I going nutty with this crazy idea that Tom Tryon was my father?

But what the fuck else was I supposed to do?

I hated my life, I hated everything I had become, all my friends were leaving me, and I was suddenly lying to my boyfriend about things we said we'd never lie about.

But I couldn't stop.

I emailed my boyfriend and lied. I told him the visit with my uncle had gone on longer than expected. I complained about my cousins and the Grand Canyon just to give the whole thing some reality. Then I left my uncle's apartment building in the morning — taking the train from New London. I took a cab to a bus that would take me to Hartford and the Tom Tryon family store.

I googled "Gay guest house Hartford" and Haut Culture came up. Of course it was run by a little old fag couple who considered themselves to be very artistic. When I got there the next day they showed me around the place, which is what faggots do with their guest houses. They're like old ladies. They will not rest until you have seen every nook and cranny of what they've "designed," which is almost always in very bad taste. And you have to compliment them, which is hard. They had a lot of tacky drawings of nude males rendered in pastels. I don't know who would like this shit. Maybe old gardening faggots. There was a painting above my bed that I guess they thought was very Andy Warhol because it was a painting of a bunch of spaghetti tins. When I finally wrenched myself free of them it was obvious I wasn't their kind of fag. I told them that I was a writer. And they asked — "would we have heard of you?" And I felt like saying, "No, I'm an old faggot novelist, and the men in my books actually have sex with each other, but it's not pornography, so of course you wouldn't have read it, you uptight pretentious nerds." I didn't say that — but when they asked me down to breakfast I said: "I don't do breakfast." *That* didn't go over very well, let me tell you.

I couldn't think about anything except Tom Tryon. It was still Sunday and the Tom Tryon family store wouldn't be open until Monday, so I had one night to stay in Hartford. I went back to the internet again. I thought for sure there must be proof Tom Tryon was a homo, I mean there must be a scorned ex-lover or something. (Look at John Travolta or Tom Cruise.) I tried "Tom Tryon gay" in a Google search. Something came up on some gay celebrity website. It said that Tom Tryon was rumoured to be gay. I knew it. And that he was also rumoured to have had an affair with Casey Donovan. Oh Jesus Christ, this was gold. Casey Donovan was one of the biggest porn stars ever, in fact he was kind of the first porn star, because he was in a movie called *Boys in the Sand* in the '60s. And Casey Donovan was a blond god of a guy to everybody in the '60s and '70s. But what a couple: Tom Tryon and Casey Donovan. Dark and light. Closeted and uncloseted. Good and evil. Wow. Talk about demon twins (i.e., *The Other*).

Somehow I found a biography of Casey Donovan on Google Books and there was an index. And Tom Tryon was in it. Tom Tryon was very closeted, especially about going out with a porn star, so they kept their relationship very secret. It said something about Tom Tryon having penthouse parties in New York City and Casey Donovan being invited, and about how Casey wanted to have a relationship with Tom, and Tom was probably in love with him but he finally ended it because . . . and then it went to a blank page. Fuck.

When I woke up the next morning I realized I didn't have the proper clothes to wear to a men's clothing store. The only proper shirt I had was dirty and sweaty from the visit to my uncle so I did a crazy thing. I wore my tank top that says "Tight End" on it. This is of course exactly the wrong thing to wear to a very straight uptight upper-class New England men's clothing store — but that just shows how unhinged I was.

The Stackpole Moore Tryon building is on a corner and it's very old and beautiful, if you're into historic architecture — lots of wood and windows. It looks down on a tree-shaded street, beside all these old office buildings — buildings that were probably skyscrapers when they were built at the beginning of the last century. The Tryon store had a sale on men's suits.

I walked in the door, which was open as it was a summer day. The air conditioning hit me like a smack in the face.

It was a palace of men. The walls were filled with larger-than-life photos of handsome models in stylish suits and perfectly fitting shirts. Impossibly handsome blonds and mysterious, dark-eyed brunettes, lounging by patios, waterfalls and plants — you know, chatting, laughing, just being together the way beautiful men always do, right? The place was actually kind of giving me a chub-on. I was at a fashion photo shoot once (I can't remember why) so I know that all the clothes on those cute models are split open and taped up at the back. Who cares? They still look hot.

A spiral staircase led to a semicircular second level. Upstairs were accessories, like hats (Do men still wear hats?), ties, and belts. So I was standing there, looking like a freak. At first it seemed like there was nobody in the store. Then a young man appeared, like out of a dream, and softly padded across the carpeted floor. He was one of those low-big-assed guys, you know what I mean?

He was young and handsome in a dark furry way and wearing a dark blue suit. The suit matched his eyes, and of course he had sexy dark stubble. I could just imagine what his body would be like. He would have a hairless torso, except for a fab treasure trail meandering down to you-know-what (he didn't trim it, he was just born that way). He wouldn't be all built up and muscly, but compact with sweet little lickable, pinchable (*Ouch, Daddy!*) tits. The main thing was I could tell his torso was so fucking long and that he would have thick, furry legs. I just love those big low-slung butts at the base of an extended, slim torso. I was sure he had the kind of body hair that just starts above the butt and goes down the legs — like a fucking satyr.

And the thing was, he was completely innocent. He was one of those straight guys (or I suppose he could have been gay) who have absolutely no guile and no clue. Not stupid, just naïve. I could tell that even though I was wearing my "Tight End" T-shirt it didn't matter to him at all, he didn't even see it. Or if he did see it, he wasn't going to judge. When he got to me I realized he was somewhat shorter than me, which was also a big turn-on. Short guys are usually attracted to me. (Or they were *once*.)

The only catch was that — at the same moment as he floated towards me like some sort of perfect-porn fantasy

— a disgusting loser also turned up. On the sleek cherry wood counter in the corner there was a computer that I guess was also a cash register. As if out of nowhere this horrible creature emerged and stood behind it. He was a faggot for sure, wearing a very natty white linen suit. The suit looked terrible on him because he was too fucking skinny for words. He also had a shaved head and a moustache. It made him look like a villain in an old Hollywood movie. And I could tell that the moment he saw me he had my number; and boy, he hated me on sight.

That's the story of my life. Gay people hate me — especially guys who wear linen suits and are trying to pretend they're normal (even though everything about them is always *super* gay). Guys like this hate me *because* I wear "Tight End" T-shirts to a fancy store. They know what I'm up to, and they hate it because it cramps their "respectable" style.

So anyway, just as this beautiful kid is approaching me, this decrepit, creepy, boring nerd spy guy is eyeing me from behind the counter. I can tell what he's thinking: "Girlfriend, if you try *anything* with that kid I'll rip your fucking balls off." So I lost it and acted like a fucking gearbox. It was the combination of the beautiful boy, Tom Tryon, and the icky old faggot who had my number.

"Welcome to Stackpole Moore Tryon," the boy said.

I told him I was glad to be here.

"And can I help you with something today, sir?"

I told him that I wanted to buy a suit for a wedding.

"A summer wedding?"

"Yes, it's next week." I lied through my teeth.

"Oh is it in Hartford? We keep up on the local betrothals."

How precocious. He said the word "betrothals." Anything this kid did impressed me.

"No," I said, "it's in Toronto."

"Oh you're from Canada?"

"Yes."

"I thought I detected a trace of an accent." Jesus what a good employee he was. What a good boy he was. I wanted to make him bad. He was standing between me and the slimy faggot who hated me. The slimy faggot was actually craning his head, standing on his tippy toes, to see what was going on.

"Would you be looking for a linen suit?" asked my polite boy.

No, I didn't want to end up looking like the monster behind the counter. "I was thinking maybe . . . seersucker?" I had no idea what seersucker was, but it had the word "suck" in it.

"Oh yes, we have some great seersucker suits." Did he put an accent the word "suck"? "Do you know your measurements?"

Oh my God, the question. The question I had been waiting for, praying for. What was happening? I had momentarily forgotten about Tom Tryon but for some reason what I was doing with this kid seemed crazily connected with my quest. "No, I don't." I tried to use my acting skills. "Sorry, I . . . ."

"No worries. I'll just get my tape." He walked away. This was going as planned, except the creature from the black lagoon behind the counter might ruin it.

When the boy came back he was playing with the tape measure in his hands. It was attached to a little metal case. He was clicking the tape measure, gently.

"So do you mind if I . . ."

I made my move, deftly, a little helpless, apologetic. "I'm sorry I . . . I'm just a little nervous about . . . getting measured . . . in public . . ."

"Oh I understand," he said, really concerned. "Some people are."

"So if you don't mind, could we go into one of the dressing rooms?"

"Yes of course, certainly." He had no idea. He led the way, padding along the floor again. I was so aroused. I didn't look back, afraid the snake in the linen suit was following us. But fuck him if he was.

I got to watch the boy's ass of course, and again, I was amazed at the sheer volume of it. A face could disappear in an ass like that. It was an ass that could kill me or something with its vastness. It was the ass that ate Hartford.

He stopped at the door of the dressing room, and said, "Here we are." I nodded a thank-you and went in. "Do you mind locking it?" I said. "Sorry to be so paranoid." There I was, acting again. He did so, suspecting nothing. There was a giant mirror in that spacious room; the room was the size of a one-bedroom apartment in Manhattan. He made the little clicking sound with the tape measure again. It was like he was warming it up, playing with it. "Extend your arms please sir?" I did. He measured one, then the other. This seemed odd to me. Are people's arms of different lengths? But nothing would make me interrupt him touching me. He would take a measurement, then put his tape measure in his pocket, then pull out a little pad, make a note, and then put the pad away and start over. He measured my neck and my chest. The chest was quite amazing. His young arms around me. I was looking directly in the mirror and I could see my head above his head and that big ass crammed into his tight blue suit in the mirror. Then he said the magic words. "Now if you don't mind . . ."

"Don't mind?"

"Sir, the inseam."

Ah yes . . . This is what the whole thing had been about from the beginning. He knew it and I knew it. We both knew. He must, right? I mean he *must*.

"Could you spread your legs a bit, sir?"

"Why of course," I said and spread them willingly. I was 62 years old and there was a hard-on bursting out of my pants. Didn't he see it? How could he not see it? It wasn't sticking straight out, it was encased in underwear, but it was throbbing, ready. As his hand approached my crotch with the tape measure, I just couldn't help it. I swear. I did it for myself, I did it for all the old fags of the world who aren't dead yet. I took his hand and placed it on my dick. He looked up at me. I didn't see anything there but wonder.

There was a knock on the door.

"Excuse me. Excuse me. What's going on in there?" It was the crazy crawfish, the ugly lobster monster of a man who wanted to ruin my fun.

"Um, we're just um . . . measuring . . ." stammered out the young man staring at me with — what seemed to me — anticipation.

"Excuse me." A harsh insistent little knock. Viperish. Petty. And effeminate in all the wrong ways. "I'm sorry but we don't do our measuring in dressing rooms at Stackpole Moore Tryon. We do our measuring on the store floor, where everybody can see." He started turning the doorknob, which was locked from the inside. He wiggled it violently. "Excuse me." He tapped again. "I would ask you to please open that door."

I swear the boy was still staring at me. The boy opened the door.

If the other salesman had been a cartoon character, the angry skinny lizard now in front of me would have had smoke coming out of his ears. I could see that, up close, his skin was disgusting — moist and gelatinous, with pockmarks, obviously the tragic harvest of tortured gay teen acne. He stamped his feet.

"I'm sorry, sir, but I'm afraid I will have to ask you to leave."

"Are you afraid?" I said, suddenly very pissed off with the stupid empty formalities of everyday speech.

He expelled air petulantly. "I don't know what you mean, but I will have to ask you to leave."

"Why? I didn't do anything wrong."

"Well, it must have been your idea to take this young man into the dressing room for this.

"Tom would never do that."

Tom. The boy's name was *Tom*.

"Well, I'm sure he didn't —" started the young man. He was going to defend me, which was pretty great considering that he knew exactly what I did and why I had asked him to go into the dressing room and lock the door.

"I repeat, it must have been his idea . . ." said the creature.

I lost it. I couldn't stand him talking anymore. I slapped him. "You're a disgusting old faggot." It felt so fucking good.

The freak didn't waste any time. He slapped me back. "That's the pot calling the kettle black."

The only thing was, whereas my slap was just a gentle stage slap — on the fat of his cheek — he was wearing a ring and it really hurt.

"Fucking Jesus Christ. What the fuck was that. You almost put my eye out."

"Get out of here. Get out of my store."

"*Greasy craterface fuck.*"

"*Fat old pervert.*"

The young man — looking very concerned and confused — was trying to drag him away from me now.

I was worried about my young man. He had touched my cock. My pulse was racing as I ran out the door of Stackpole Moore Tryon to hide in the doorway of a greasy spoon across the street. I didn't want the crazed skinny swamp thing to hit me on the face with his ring again. I peered around the corner of the doorway to see if I was being followed.

He wasn't there. But my young man was standing just outside the doorway of Stackpole Moore Tryon. What was going on? Did he miss me? I leaned out of the doorway of the greasy spoon and gestured for him to come over. He acknowledged me with a nod and then hurried across the street until he was in front of me.

"I'm sorry, sir," he said. He was sorry for me, and I had just molested him. Go figure. Did this mean he was sexually attracted to me? Fuck, I hoped so.

"Jesus Christ, I don't like that guy," I said, cradling my face.

"Let me see?" I removed my hand. He touched my face. "You're getting a bit of a bruise," he said.

"I shouldn't have yelled," I said.

"Yeah, but that ring is like a weapon, sir." Why was he so reasonable? Why are some young men so reasonable, even when you molest them?

"Look, I have to get back to the store, I just wanted to make sure you were all right."

I really wanted to kiss him, but I remembered the incident with Nathaniel and thought better of it. But if he went away without me asking him about Tom Tryon then my whole trip to Hartford would be for nothing.

"Listen, sorry, can I ask you a question?"

"Yes, sure." His young, eager face turned to mine.

"I'm trying to get in touch with someone from the Tryon family." He looked at me blankly. "You know, of Stackpole Moore Tryon."

"Oh right, he said. "We pronounce it Try*On*, with the accent on the second syllable."

That was odd.

"Do you know if any of the Try*On*s are still around?"

"Well, there's one here."

"Where?" I asked.

"Here," he said, pointing into the greasy spoon.

"You mean in this restaurant?"

"Yes," he said. "Lane. Lane Tryon. He works here."

"Is that Tom Tryon's brother?"

"I'm not sure. But his dad used to own the store."

That was Tom Tryon's brother. "What's he doing working here?"

"I don't know. But this is where he works."

Jesus. I had stumbled onto a gold mine.

"I have to get back," he said. "My boss will be really angry."

"I'm sorry I caused you so much trouble."

"No trouble . . ." he said. "See you later."

And he was gone.

I stepped outside to look at the name on the restaurant. It was called the Cubbyhole and the sign said "Since 1952." So this place had been around since Tom Tryon lived in Hartford and knew my mother. Maybe they had eaten lunch here.

I walked in. A man was standing behind a little lectern that said, "Welcome."

The restaurant was pretty obviously old, but in good

condition. It was tiny — only six little tables and a small counter. It was a relic.

So was the man behind the lectern.

He was taller than me, probably six-foot-two. He was pretty gigantic. He was fat but not round, a big chest and a hanging belly. He had dark straight hair, a moustache and a beard, and a large, smiling, welcoming face. But he was much older than me, he looked like he must be in his late 70s — sagging jowls and lines were carved into his tanned skin. But the first thing anyone would notice about him was his voice.

It was the gayest voice I have ever heard. There's swishy, and there's pinched effeminate, like the lizard clerk in Stackpole Moore Tryon. Then there's just all-out gay. We're talking swish beyond swish, gluey and oozy, chock full of innuendo. A voice that drips with winks and double-entendres. We're talking about somebody who literally can't open his mouth without something camp or flirtatious falling out. We're talking One Hundred Percent Faggot.

"Well, well, well," he said, sizing me up from head to toe. "What can I do for you, mister?"

I was surprised he didn't call me sailor, but I had a feeling that would happen soon.

"Can I give you a little help? Coffee, tea, or me?" He held the menus in front of his crotch in what was intended to be an alluring fashion.

"I'm hoping you can help me," I said, trying to sound as neutral and un-gay as possible. Guys like him always do that to me. I mean I'm effeminate, I know I am, but nothing like this one.

"I'm looking for some information about the Try*On* family."

I put the accent on the second syllable.

"You mean *Try*on?"

"Yes — they told me to put the accent on the second syllable across the street."

"Pretentious bastards." He looked at me demurely. "You look a bit too grown-up to be doing a school project, honey."

"I'm interested in learning more about Tom Tryon," I said.

He batted his eyelashes at me. "My big brother."

"Tom Tryon was your brother? Are you Lane Tryon?"

"Guilty as charged." He had a bit of a speech impediment, as if he was talking with something heavy and wet in his mouth, inhibiting his tongue. "How can I help you, Mr. Man?

"Do you want to sit down? How would you like a big, juicy mouth-watering . . . burger?"

He must have turned that straightforward question into a come-on about a thousand times.

"I get off in half an hour. If you want to wait for me . . . sailor . . . I'll take you up to my place and we can chat." He said the word chat the way someone else might say *blow job*. How was I going to defend myself against this guy? He was an old man. I mean I was old, but he was really old. There was absolutely nothing attractive about him. And he was obviously very attracted to me. How was I going to keep out of his clutches, but get information about his brother Tom?

Right now I just wanted to make sure he talked to me.

"Sure," I said. I was actually sounding a lot more masculine than I ever have — and feeling that way too. This guy would make anyone feel like a man. "Sure, I'll have a burger and then we can talk."

"Sounds fab, Mr. Handsome. Let me get you a seat." He

gave a little Marilyn Monroe swivel to his hips and gestured for me to follow him into the restaurant. He sat me at a large booth. There was no one else in the restaurant, except an older man sitting at the counter sipping a soda. Was it a gay place? It seemed to me that they probably wouldn't have a gay restaurant in Hartford, but a waiter like this would make any place gay.

"Do you know what you want?" he asked, his leering voice booming.

"I'll just have a cheeseburger, fries, and a shake," I said.

"Excellent choice. I'm going to take special care of you, mister, don't you worry."

He tapped the menu on the table and swished away.

This didn't make any sense. Or did it? Tom Tryon having a younger gay brother who was the gayest man who ever lived. How could that be? Would it have emboldened Tom to have an out-of-the-closet younger brother? Or did the whole thing work in another way? I thought about how in some families, the younger brother was a pale imitation of the older brother, who was considered first in line to the throne. Even in my family, my uncle was called "Sonny" by my grandparents, and my own father was kind of the assistant brother, in second place. My father's actions didn't matter quite as much, because his older brother was the centre of all the family attention. If Tom Tryon was the first brother, the important brother, then it would be a lot harder for him to be gay than for his younger brother.

But still . . . this? Such a flamer in such a small city? But then I remembered that it was pretty much in smaller places like this that you find the real old-fashioned faggots. They kind of become the "town queer," and sometimes people accept them for that. After all, when you're as gay as this guy in a city the size of Hartford, there would be no point in hiding it.

He was back. "Your water, sir," he said. "It's hot day out there . . . and I know how you big men sweat."

"I'm not that big." Why did I say that? I was trying to turn this into a non-flirt thing but I had just opened up a discussion on my "bigness."

"Oh, you look pretty big to me, honey. And I know about these things. You know what they say — big shoes, big feet." He cackled wildly at his own joke. "Pardon my French." He whooped and flapped his hand around. "Your burger will be ready in a jiff, and then I'll cash out, if you know what I mean."

Yes I did know what he meant, but I didn't get the innuendo. However, I tried to smile politely just because everything he did and said seemed to imply *something*. Wow. My own smile suddenly reminded me of the one the boy gave me at Stackpole Moore Tryon. Trapped into responding to the advances of someone to whom you have no sexual attraction. But I wasn't like this old lecherous fag, was I? All this made me think about being in the very tough position of needing someone who is coming on to you, and therefore not wanting to appear rude by showing your disgust with them. It suddenly occurred to me that some people sleep with people they aren't attracted to, just to get stuff, or worse yet, just to be *nice*.

After Lane sashayed over with my burger, he winked at me and told me he would be back to pick me up in a minute.

It was a good burger. There were little mirrors beside the booth and I caught a glimpse of my face. There was a bruise at the right side of my eye where the skinny freak at Stackpole Moore Tryon had slapped me. I was surprised that Lane hadn't noticed. I finished my burger, and a young girl — I guess Lane's shift replacement — came out and took away my plate. "Lane will be with you in a minute," she said.

Lane turned up in front of me just as I was making a large

sucking sound with a straw, cleaning up the end of the milk-shake.

"Good, isn't it?" he said. "They use the real stuff here. Everywhere else they use some sort of fake milk beverage, but here at the Cubbyhole, we use real actual cream. Nothing like *real cream*, honey." He smacked his lips. "Shall we go?"

"Sure," I said, feeling like a young, masculine prostitute. It wasn't a bad feeling, but it was weird.

He led me out and then turned quickly to a little dilapi-dated doorway beside the restaurant entrance. He opened the door with a key and there was a steep old wooden stairway in front of us. "I'm up on the second floor," he said. So, he lived above the Cubbyhole.

I followed his massive ass up the stairs. Only it wasn't the kind of massive ass I liked. It was the ass of an old woman — the huge, sagging cheeks were flat and the crack of his big old butt was swallowing the back of his shorts. I tried to look away but there was really nowhere to look. When we got to the landing it was very hard to stand beside him without touching him but somehow I managed it. "Welcome to Chez Lane," he said.

He opened the door.

He led me into a sitting room that took up the whole floor, but wasn't very big. I figured this room was his whole apartment. It was a bit smaller than the Cubbyhole, which was pretty small.

It looked like an old lady's apartment, which I guess in a way it was. There were little knickknacks everywhere, china dogs, Blue Mountain Pottery figures, and old worn lacey fabrics on the arms of the chairs. There was an old TV table in front of the couch with a painting of horses on it. (Remember TV tables?) There were also stacks of old books and newspapers against the walls, and what looked to me like photo albums. Maybe there were pictures of my mother and Tom Tryon in them. Maybe.

"Sit down and make yourself comfortable. Relax," he said. "It's not a palace, but it does the job if you know what I mean." Again an innuendo with no clear meaning — or maybe a meaning that was too scary for me to think about. Did he think I came up here for a blow job? Did I look that desperate? I figured I'd better get to the point.

"I'm writing a book about Tom Tryon," I lied.

"Is it fiction or non-fiction?" he said.

"I'm going to tell the truth as I see it," I said.

"Then it's fiction, honey. Let me tell you, I've been around the block a few times, and it's all fiction. Would you like a drink?"

"No thank you."

"Well, I'm going to have one, hope you don't mind. After a long hard day at the Cubbyhole I sure as hell need one." He gestured to me to sit down on the couch. He sat in the big La-Z-Boy that was opposite an old TV, thank God. There was another TV table beside the chair with a bottle of gin and a glass on it. "My day starts at 6 a.m., so even though it's noon it feels like I've worked a whole day. So what makes you so interested in Tom Tryon?"

"Well, I don't know if you're aware, but New York Review Books just reissued *The Other*, and I read it, and I thought it was —"

"That book was about me."

"What?"

"I said it was about me. You don't believe me? I was the evil brother. Or *he* was. Or we *both* were. It's all very complicated. Tom was very complicated. Are you sure you don't want a drink? You might need one."

"No, no thank you."

"Tom's story is tragic. Oh so tragic. I've told it many times. You're not the only person who's threatened to write a book about him. But the truth is there is a part of the family — the part of the family that is still connected to Stackpole Moore Tryon — who aren't too eager to let that story out. There's a lot of closet cases still around, you know. But I'm sure you know. A big guy like you looks like he knows the score and has covered the waterfront, if you get my drift. Now me, I'm not a closet case, never was. That was the problem with me. I've got the kind of a mouth that was made to suck dick, honey, and all I have to do is say hello and people know. It makes some of them uncomfortable, you know what I mean? What about you?"

He was drinking the gin neat, no ice, no mix, no nothing. "What?"

"The fact that I'm a good cocksucker — does it make you uncomfortable?"

I didn't want to sound uptight, but I didn't want him sucking my dick. What to do? But I sure *did* want to know whether or not Tom Tryon was my father.

"Umm . . . no . . ."

"That's good, because I'd sure like to suck your cock honey."

I didn't know what to say.

"Can I ask you some questions . . . first?" Why did I say "first"?

"Oh, you're amenable. I like a man who is amenable. And you're so easy on the eyes. I also like a man who's easy on the eyes. I can tell you've got a nice one."

I cleared my throat. "But I do want to hear about Tom . . ."

"Tom, Tom, Tom — everyone wants to hear about Tom.

Well, sometimes I get tired of talking about him. From the start he was the special one. I was the black sheep of the family because I climbed out of my mother's womb sucking cock. And you know what's amazing? Tom was just as queer as me. Queerer in fact. I mean, when he got all revved up he was the nelliest queen you've ever seen. But it looked bad for him to hang out with me because I blew his cover — and all his friends — because everyone could tell what a fag I was. So like in *The Other*, I was the evil twin. I mean we weren't twins but — whatever. I mean back then we looked like we were twins. I was very handsome in my day, though I know you don't believe it. In fact this is what Tom Tryon would have looked like if he hadn't have died of stomach cancer in 1995." He leaned over and waved his hand around dismissively. "Stomach cancer. Right. He died of AIDS. He died of AIDS like everybody else. I don't know why I didn't get it. I'm sure I sucked more cock than he did. I mean, Tom was very shy, didn't want people to know, so he had to rely on his good looks, which got him laid, as I can tell you. But me, I would just go up to people and say, can I do ya, honey? And there's something about my mouth. I'll take your whole bait and tackle, balls and all, and you'll have a really good time coming in my mouth, you really will."

It was like every time he started talking about Tom Tryon, Lane ended up talking about my cock in his mouth. I tried to change the subject.

"Was Casey Donovan the real love of Tom's life?"

"Casey, Casey, Casey. What a doll, what a living doll he was. Great cock too, I sucked him once believe it or not, and he had a fabulous cock with a big knob on the end, you know, one with big a ridge on it you can really get your mouth around — and the head kind of hangs over the rest of the cock like it's a giant vegetable or something."

"Was Tom in love with Casey?"

"I think he thought he was. But he couldn't handle it. When he met Casey, Tom was trying to make it as a big Hollywood movie star, and of course then — like now — you couldn't be a big Hollywood movie star and also suck the big cock. *No*, couldn't do that. Times haven't changed much, have they? So he lived in L.A. but he would have these penthouse parties in New York City, and then he'd be in love with Casey while the party was on and crying and writing me letters, he used to write me letters, and he'd pour out his heart to me in those letters, and I have them. If you want to read them, if you want to publish them, you can have them. My brother felt sorry for me because he knew I got the short end of the stick, but I didn't have the short end really, if you get my meaning. But anyway, he felt sorry for Lane, so he would send me these letters where he would tell me everything, and I want them out there. I want to see those fucking letters published. I don't give a fuck about my uncle's part of the family. They rooked me out of the family business because I'm a fucking faggot, so fuck them. Fuck them. You might as well tell the whole world about Tom Tryon and his fucking fellatio-dillos . . ."

I think he meant to say peccadillos. But I tried to get him back on track. "Tom was married, right?"

"Oh God yes, for three years. She was a fucking witch. She was his beard, and it was torture for him. I told him not to get married . . . and she tried to take him for all he had, and she did, you know, she could — because he was so scared of what she might say about him. God, we both hated her . . ."

"Were there any other women?"

"Not that I know of . . . there were no women . . . Tom didn't like women, well, he liked them fine, but not in *that* way. But you know I have a theory. I always got along with women a lot better than Tom because you know when you're forced to marry one, when you're forced to marry a woman, and live with her, and maybe even fuck her — and I think he actually fucked Ann Noyes, don't know why, out of guilt I guess, trying to prove he was a man, he was very fucked up — but anyway when you're forced to live in a closeted situation like that one and you have to pretend you love women, then you get *not* to like them. I always loved women. You know, there are women who come all the way from New London just to have lunch at the Cubbyhole and not because they like the food — though the food's not bad — but because they like *me*. Fuck they *love* me. I make them all feel like queens. Women just want to be treated like beautiful queens, that's all they want, and I *do* treat them that way, plus give them a little laugh with their club sandwiches, and they love it *all* honey, they love it *all*."

"So there was no one that was the love of his life? The secret love that he didn't tell anybody about? I mean did he . . ." I was going to ask if there had possibly been a child out of wedlock — in other words, me. But he interrupted my train of thought.

"Well," he said, and there was a wry smile on his face, "there was . . . Pat."

Pat. I froze. Pat was my mother's name.

"What Pat? A woman named Pat?"

"Well, I'm almost sure Pat was a man. Pat would have had to be a man. I just call him Pat. His real name was Patrick Norton. If an imaginary person can have a real name, or was

Patrick Norton imaginary?" He put his fat hairy fingers to his lips. "You gotta wonder . . ."

"Please . . . what are you talking about?"

"Don't get your titties in a twist, honey. Because they *do* look like nice titties to me."

I didn't want to be rude. "I just really need to know who this Patrick Norton is."

"Oh, it's the name he used. The name he used for his *perfect lover*. I first heard about it from one of his friends at one of Tom's parties. Oh yes, Tom used to invite me to his parties. They were wild things. And it wasn't a huge place. It wasn't a loft like they have nowadays. Don't you just love the faggots with their lofts? No dear, it was just a walk-up in an old brownstone on the East Side, but when you went up the steps to the main floor, there was this huge living room all done up in red, like an old whorehouse, with fringes on the lampshades and big red chairs, Persian carpets, the whole bit, and there was a bed, in the living room — only it was on stilts, you know, what do they call it, like, a loft bed — even though as I say it wasn't a loft — and the bathroom off the living room. It was like a little sex palace, the walls of that bathroom were covered with dirty pictures from gay magazines and people used to go in there and fuck. And then you went upstairs and the kitchen and bathroom were all done up with barn wood like a Provincetown weekend with potted palms, and there was deck and several bedrooms up there. I don't know whose apartment that was — it wasn't Tom's. He rented it every six months or so for his parties. Anyway, there was a lot of action at those parties. Of course it was better than a bathhouse, and I would just go out on the deck and install myself out there and all the lost drunken horny souls would wander out — and some were very pretty models, let me tell you — and they would all end up on that deck eventually and I would have them moaning and wriggling around like their lives depended on it.

"Well, this one model boy — after I gave him a blow job he'd never forget — started talking about Tom, saying that Tom was all depressed. And I asked him why and I said, 'It's his party and he can cry if he wants to,' and he said, 'Yeah, well he is, he's mad at Casey.' Which was always a huge problem at these parties — because the parties were organized so that he could fuck Casey somewhere, when they were high, in one of those bedrooms upstairs near the barn wood kitchen, without guilt, or whatever. I don't know, my brother was *so* fucked up around sex I can barely think about it. Anyway, after this lovely kid came in my mouth, he goes on about Tom and Casey's little spat. I can't remember the details. It was always the same anyway, Tom being jealous and insecure — my brother didn't have a secure bone in his body. So the kid says, 'Casey went home and now Tom is going on and on about Patrick Norton.' And I asked him who the fuck Patrick Norton was. And he said, 'Patrick Norton — his imaginary lover.' And I said, 'What the fuck is an imaginary lover?' And the kid said, 'He's the perfect man and he only exists in Tom's dreams and sometimes Tom writes stories about him.'"

Well, that was certainly interesting, but I was very disappointed to find out that Pat was Patrick Norton and not my mother. I thought that maybe there was still a chance that in all those letters and photographs — at least that's what I thought they were — piled against the walls, I might find a picture of Tom Tryon with my mother. Or maybe even Tom Tryon holding me as a baby.

I mean you never know.

"Are those photo albums? On the floor over there?"

"They might be."

"Would you mind if I had a look at them?"

"What do I get out of it?"

"Um . . ." I had to play this card right. "I would be *very* thankful," I said.

Oh Jesus. I really was a whore.

"Then do anything you like, honey. I'm just going to watch a little TV."

This didn't really make any sense. But nothing in this whole scene did. Lane settled himself in his easy chair and turned on the remote. I could hear what sounded like '70s disco music coming out of the TV but I was obsessed with the photo albums. I opened one up and I could see right away that they were very conveniently labelled. One said "Tom as Texas John Slaughter" and it had all sorts of pictures of Tom on the set for the TV show, standing beside his horse, holding his 10-gallon hat in his hand, his arm around a very pretty actress — or was that his wife Anne? — and with what looked like his parents. There was a man standing with Tom's parents who looked like Tom but was a little bit fatter and not quite as handsome. It was Lane. It's amazing the way some people age (and some don't). I could see how you might have seen the two of them together at that age, like my Uncle Charlie obviously had, and thought — "Wow, those are two handsome twin brothers." But if you looked at Tom you could see there was just something leaner and hungrier about him. And it wasn't just about body fat. He was tortured, he was fucked up, he was just not comfortable in his own skin. Lane was a bit looser, messier, already slightly going to seed. Lane was Tom without the anguish.

I flipped through a couple of other Hollywood-style albums and then there was one labelled "The Beach." Sure enough, it was Osprey. And there was Tom in his bathing suit looking dreamy as hell and Lane smiling sort of crook-edly and looking a bit pudgy. I looked and looked. Finally I found one picture that was of my mother for sure. It was Tom Tryon and my mother and Camilla Wilson. At least it was Tom and he had his arm around two beautiful girls, one a blond (Camilla) and one a brunette (my mother). They were standing in their bathing suits in front of a sign that said "London" and "Paris" — with arrows going this way and that. It must have been some sort of joke sign that was near the beach or near New London somewhere. They all looked very beautiful, and Tom was smiling, which wasn't usual in these photographs. It was a clue; but it wasn't a jackpot.

Then I hit the jackpot. I opened an album marked "Letters," just for the hell of it, and a whole bunch of letters fell out. These must have been the letters that Lane had talked about. The ones that he wanted to see published. But what I saw there stopped me in my tracks. Suddenly I wasn't interested in any of the other letters anymore, or any of the photos, because one of the letters that fell out had some drawings attached to it. They were the same drawings that I'd found so many days ago as part of my mother's memorabilia.

The cartoons were very distinctive. There was no doubt about it, these were drawn in exactly the same style. These letters were addressed to Lane, so instead of the handsome young man and the girl, there were caricatures of the two brothers. But Tom was represented in the same way, as a very handsome nerd (in some of the cartoons he was even wearing glasses). Lane was drawn very interestingly — as kind of already going to fat, and with an evil look in his eye. But Tom was every inch the young innocent hero. And the inscrutable signature I had noticed on the cartoons before?

It wasn't an H. It was two conjoined *T*s.

This clinched it. My mother's cartoon letters were definitely from Tom Tryon. Tom Tryon had been courting my mother and had written her love letters. Did I need any more proof?

"Can I borrow these letters?" I asked. As I got up, I could see that Lane was still sitting in his chair. He had his hand in his pants. And it was pretty clear to me what was going on. From where I was standing I could see what was on the TV by just stretching my head around. It was porn. Some very old porn. Skinny guys with moustaches. Jesus. Was that Casey Donovan? I didn't care. I realized that looking at the porn might give Lane the wrong idea. It did. He unzipped his pants and pulled out his cock.

"You like what you see, honey? You want a little slurp ramp action?" There was nothing wrong with his dick, except it wasn't big enough for a man his size. And the head of it was too red and it just . . . the more I looked at it the more disgusted I was. It's just no fun looking at someone's erect cock when you aren't sexually attracted in the least. I had the pile of letters in my hand.

"Hey, well," I said awkwardly, "there you are . . ."

"Yeah there I am, honey, and I'm all ready for you." The words tumbled out of his drunken, wet, slurpy lips. No, I did not want to suck this ugly old man's cock. I looked to the left, the door to the outside was almost within reach. I had a pile of letters in my hand. Maybe there were more letters. Maybe there were more photos. But I couldn't stay in the room anymore with this guy or I might end up letting him suck me off just so he wouldn't feel bad.

"Sorry, I gotta go," I said, turning the knob on the door.

"Hey wait," he said. The door slammed behind me. I could hear him in the room shouting and then heard the door opening. "Hey, hey what are you doing, where are you going? Are you going to say no to the best blow job in Connecticut? Hey, those are my letters. You give them back."

Well, I thought, you didn't seem too concerned about the letters before, did you?

The End

I don't know what to do because the story is over and I discovered that Tom Tryon is my real father.

What a revelation, eh? What a life changer. To be living your whole life thinking one person is your father, and then to find out that — your dream of dreams — someone else is. This could give Sarah Polley a run for her money, couldn't it? I mean after that, you would think that all my problems would be solved. I would know who I was, and feel at home with who I was, and I would become a better person, maybe make some new friends, and gain back some old ones, and stop lying to my boyfriend. Right?

Well, it didn't happen exactly like that. And the thing is, I have a confession to make. I know this whole book has been a confession, so why do I say that? Because . . . well, I don't know how to break this to you. I'm really afraid that you'll think I'm a liar. And I'm not. I don't lie about the important things.

It's like with my boyfriend and the apartment, that was a lie, and it would really make him mad if he found out that I was using the apartment in Toronto to have sex in. But, you know the difference between a big lie and a little lie? I mean we all do it, we all say, "That's just a little lie and it won't matter because I'm not *really* lying because I'm not doing the big lie." It would be a big lie to my boyfriend if, in fact, I was no longer in love with him and I was looking for a new boyfriend and I didn't tell him but instead just went and dumped him after finding a replacement. But it wasn't like that at all. When I used the apartment to fuck that photographer without telling my boyfriend, I was just doing a bad, inconvenient thing that might come back to bite both of us (the photographer might come stalk me at the apartment someday). I wasn't in love with the photographer and I didn't want to leave my boyfriend. So yes, it was a lie, but it was a little lie and it didn't matter because it didn't have anything to do with the much larger truth, which is that I love my boyfriend and I always will.

You understand the difference between a little lie and a big lie, right?

Little lies don't matter.

So the fact of the matter is that I told a little lie here. I know that it might feel like a betrayal because I promised to tell you the truth and I went on and on about how this was not going to be a piece of fiction and everything. But the truth is,

I got carried away, okay? And I got carried away in a good way, that is, I just got so involved with my own big truth, the important truth, so much so that it just seemed that the best way to make it stick would be to embellish it a little bit. What I'm saying is basically the same as what Picasso meant when he said, "Art is a lie that tells the truth." And I know you might say — and I understand why — that truth is truth. A chair is a chair. I mean it makes a difference when you go to sit down, because if you went to sit down and a chair wasn't a chair then you'd fall on the floor and it would hurt, right? But when people talk about truth, they don't understand that there is a difference between objects and concepts. Yes, there is a day-to-day truth that you need to understand so you don't end up sitting on the floor by mistake. Yes, chairs are real and you can touch them and sit on them. That's because they're objects. On the other hand, when it comes to concepts — ideas — the truth is something that is a little bit harder to define and it might be a mixture of fact and fiction. Don't ask me why — that's just the way it is.

I know, I'm stalling. I'm afraid to tell you this because I'm afraid you'll hate me — I mean you paid your money right? You paid something like $20 for this, unless you downloaded a pirated e-book or somehow cobbled together all the random pages on Google. But no matter whether you paid for this book or not, we had a deal. I started out by saying I was going to tell the whole truth and nothing but — if the whole thing turns out to be a lie — what the fuck?

It's not a lie, I promise. Okay, here is the larger truth about this book, the important one. This is what I want you to know so that you won't worry about me. (Even if I am a sad old faggot.) The truth is that in lots of ways I don't feel like the child of my parents or even a child of this world because I am such a freak and I don't fit in. I mean, even if I'm gay, couldn't I just be the kind of "nice" gay man who settles down and goes to church and has kids? But I won't do that. You see, what I finally realized after going through all the bad things I did and then thinking that maybe Tom Tryon was my father was: somehow I had to learn to be happy with who I am (as much as it sounds like Dorothy tapping her shoes together to get home, it's true). As I said to a friend the other day, "I think I'm becoming that old guy who hangs around in gay restaurants and chats up the waiters." But you know, instead of hating myself for that, I'm embracing it. Because if Tom Tryon was my father, all it would mean was that I was meant to be in this world, that I have a place in it, and I'm not alone. No matter how alone it seems that I am. I belong. To something. To the world. To me.

That's it.

So I still haven't told you what the lie is, but that's only because I'm afraid of pissing you off. In the interest of full disclosure then, here it is:

Tom Tryon is not my father.

Okay. There. I said it. Yeah, well, probably you figured it out. (I guess I'm not really good-looking enough when it comes down to it to be Tom Tryon's son. I know. I get it.)

Please don't hate me.

Does it help to tell you that not only is this a little lie because it's really based on the truth, but it's a little lie based on an even more bizarre truth than the one I made up?

Tom Tryon didn't write cartoon letters to my mother in real life. But someone else did.

I'm going to tell you the real truth now. It's like when somebody tells you the story about the dachshund that ate the whole body of the old woman who owned her because when the woman died, no one found the body for two weeks. Now if you heard that story, you wouldn't believe it, right? A dachshund eating a whole woman? But it's true. It happened. Or, if you go to: http://blogs.discovermagazine .com/gnxp/2010/08/1-in-200-men-direct-descendants-of-genghis-khan you will find out that 1 in 200 people are direct descendants of Genghis Khan. Real facts sound impossible when you first hear them, right? In fact the *more* real they are the more *impossible* they actually sound.

Anyway, here goes.

The whole truth is, and it's nothing but the truth, so help me God: my mother used to date Mr. Dressup. And there was — at one time — the thinnest, smallest, but nevertheless the *realest* chance that I could have been Mr. Dressup's son.

Yeah . . . really.

You see, when my mother was young in Connecticut, she went to school with Ernie Coombs, who grew up to be the Canadian TV celebrity Mr. Dressup. Mr. Dressup had a Canadian kids' show from the '60s to the '90s, and he used to open the "tickle trunk" and put on items of clothing to entertain the kids (and some of those items were pretty girly). A couple of generations of Canadian kids were brought up on Mr. Dressup, and towards the end of her life my mother told me that she had known Mr. Dressup in high school, and that he had been in love with her, but he had been a little skinny nerd at the time (he remained a skinny nerd all his life — just watch reruns of the show, you'll see) so she hadn't been at all romantically interested in him when she was a teenager. But much later, when she was in her 70s, my mother heard that Ernie's wife had died. So she decided to write Ernie Coombs a letter to see if he would date her on the rebound from his wife — after she had rejected him nearly 60 years earlier. Of course, my mother's little scheme didn't work. Ernie Coombs sent her a nice letter saying that he was too busy recovering from the death of his wife to date anybody. I really respected him for that. I mean if it had been me, I would have said — "Fuck you bitch, you didn't want me when I was an ugly teenaged nobody, but 60 years later I'm an ugly somebody with a dead wife and all of a sudden *now* you want me? Fuck you."

On the one hand this anecdote may shed a little more light on my origins. After all, I'm a sad old faggot, and my mother sure was a sad old straight woman, trying a stunt like this before she died. A stunt that was insulting to Ernie Coombs and the memory of his wife, and insulting to herself. But the point is: I still do actually have the cartoons that Ernie Coombs sent to my mom when he was wooing her as a teenager, and they are pictures of a little nerdy guy who looks like Ernie Coombs, bringing my mum ("Patsy") flowers and stuff, and the drawings are very funny and touching. Don't believe me? Well, if you want to see them just email me at gilbertschuyler@gmail.com. I've scanned them. You can look at the real letters from Mr. Dressup to my mother if you want.

What's the point of me telling you all this? When I heard that my mother had had a romance with Mr. Dressup, I told some of my friends and they said, "That would explain a lot." Meaning, since I'm a drag queen, that maybe if Ernie Coombs (with his tickle trunk and the feather boas) was my *real* father it would explain my addiction to drag.

No, Ernie Coombs wasn't my real father. But it got me to thinking about Tom Tryon and that's where the whole "search for my real father" story began.

Okay, so I didn't find cartoons in Lane Tryon's apartment that proved Tom Tryon was my dad. I'm sorry to get you to the happy ending and then tell you that it was made up, but can you trust me when I say that the end of my story *is* happy? That's the point of this book. Even though my father (who died recently) was my father, and he was a manager and briefly a vice president of the Travelers Insurance Company, and we had almost nothing in common — I'm okay. I mean it was tough when my dad died because everybody kept telling me how sad it was for me. But let's be real here. My father was 90 years old, and I loved him as much as you can love a dad with whom you have absolutely nothing in common. But despite having a father who was always very distant from me, I can accept me, or have figured out a way to accept me and go on about my life in a not too particularly self-destructive manner.

Or at least, I just *go on*.

Okay, if you're not buying the "Little lie to prove a real truth" thing, then maybe it will help if I talk about my boyfriend. If you're skeptical, maybe it's because I keep talking about being alone, and facing things alone. What's that all about if I have a boyfriend?

I mean do I actually *have* a boyfriend?

If I'm supposedly in love with this boyfriend and he's the love of my life and my soul mate, how could I write a whole book (which is dedicated to him) about my life and hardly mention him? How could I go around having sex with all these people and feeling up boys and kissing guys and all the rest of it when I'm supposedly in love with him? How could I not share my problems with him and count on him to solve them?

Well, I'm not going to answer those questions. I mean if you don't get it, then you don't get it. But I will say that a lot of the problem is homophobia. I want you to really think about this — even if you're gay. Doesn't it still seem, to most people, maybe even you gay guys, just a little bit unnatural for one guy to be in love with another guy? I mean it's one thing for them to do the dirty in an alley, and not tell any-body, and wipe the shit off their dicks if they're closet cases (gay guys have clean assholes, how many times do I have to tell you?). I mean, we all understand dirty gay sex, and to some degree accept it — dirty gay sex in an alley, sure. It happens. Like death and worms.

But what about the transcendent "I'm buying you flowers, and you're special, and every day I think of you, and you are my sunshine, my only sunshine" type of love? Can we really, any of us, actually believe that one guy feels that way about another guy and on top of that, that it's natural?

I don't think so.

That brings me back to the whole "Patrick Norton" thing.

Patrick Norton was Tom Tryon's name for his imaginary lover. But the thing is, nobody really knew if Patrick Norton was only someone he made up, or was ever a real person.

I'm pretty sure he was both.

Which means that you will never believe that I have a boyfriend, or that I am in love with my boyfriend, or that we have been lovers for 17 years, and that we have an open relationship, and that he is my ideal life partner. You might believe that I am deluding myself into believing that a friend that I fuck now and then or once fucked is my lover, and I'm living in a state of delusion, and that I'm a screwed up pro-miscuous homosexual who has an old friend who he likes to think is his love and his partner, but that's just very sad. And it's especially sad that I would write a whole book that is sup-posedly about him but is not really about him in which I fuck a lot of other people. What's that about?

The point of all this can be boiled down to one question: how can I be in love with somebody when no one believes that I am in love with them?

Well, let me tell you this . . . And it's all true . . .

My lover, Patrick Norton, is tall, slim and handsome, and has sparkling eyes. He understands everything I say before I say it. He makes me laugh. He has a benign hold over me, which means he rules my life with a firm but gentle hand. He loves me very much and admires me but I admire him more. He is heroic. He does heroic things for people who are underprivileged and works to make the world a better place. He believes the world can be changed and he fights for what he believes in, even though he often won't admit what a hero he is. He won't take any bullshit from me, but he would also fight anyone to the death who tried to hurt me. He is brave. He is fearless. But of course I love him and protect him when he needs it too and when I can. But most of all he can deal with life. Which in case you haven't figured it out from reading this — I can't.

So you can say that's all a lie and a delusion and I know you will. Or maybe you got the point of all this and you realize that it's true.

Finally, Really

Finally, really, last week I met the perfect fuck buddy. I'm not sure if we will ever meet again, but if it's not him, I'm sure there is someone else out there like him who is perfect for an old guy like me. He's probably in his 40s and I met him at the baths. His name is Joe (I actually asked him his name, which is a big thing for me as I'm sure you know by now). He is furry all over and has a great big cock and a perfectly muscled body. He's short. He has a beard. He's very handsome and submissive. All he likes to do is hold me down, worship my body, and suck my cock until I come. I think he will solve all of my problems.

Well okay, maybe not all of them.